THE WRECK OF ECHO 10-4

THE SHOOTING SCRIPT

RYAN CAVANAGH
LINA APICELLA
AUSTIN PARENTI
PHILIP KING

NOBLE ROGUE
PUBLISHING

To *The Wreck of Echo 10-4* crew,
a determined group of creatives
who labored through a South Florida
summer to make this film a reality.

FOREWORD

The hardest day on *The Fountain of Youth* was at Giacomo Tanti's mansion. The July sun beat us down as we captured Val's slow-motion rescue. We each looked for any excuse to go inside the home and hide from the blazing heat.

That day, I observed two people on the crew who outworked me: Lina Apicella and Ryan Cavanagh. Our cinematographer Zach Guinta told me how impressed he was with those two. I immediately replied, "That's why they're directing with me next summer." I didn't know exactly what I meant at the time. But I knew whatever we would do the following year, I wanted them at the helm.

A few months later, in the fall of 2021, I invited Lina and Ryan to join Philip King and me in the writers' room for our next project. We knew we wanted to make a four-part series, but we had yet to decide on a story. In one of our earliest meetings, King inspired us with a concept: an air force veteran who fakes his death to avoid the mob and his nagging wife. We mapped out the story and partitioned our episodes. Echo 10-4 was born.

As the scripts came together and pre-production began, I feared we bit off more than we could chew. The story required double the action, triple the cast, and quadruple the visual effects as Fountain. Would this project be our doom? Or would it be another great leap forward in Studio 70's history?

Production was a blur. We filmed a bus heist, sky dive, plane crash, bus crash, cop chase, dirt bike chase, and more in less than two months. Ironically, after all that craziness, our final shot was an empty couch in a quiet living room.

The Wreck of Echo 10-4 was intensely challenging. I sometimes catch myself wondering how on earth we managed it! Then I remind myself of the answer: Lina Apicella, Ryan Cavanagh, Philip King, and the rest of our extraordinary crew. It is an absolute privilege to know these mighty and talented young filmmakers. Their fierce determination brought *The Wreck of Echo 10-4* to life.

Sincerely yours,

Austin Parenti

THE WRECK OF ECHO 10-4

Written by

Ryan Cavanagh
Lina Apicella
Austin Parenti
Philip King

8401 Belvedere Road
West Palm Beach, FL 33411
(516)639-5636

THE WRECK OF ECHO 10-4

EXT. SKY - DAY

Blue skies and white clouds. Suddenly, a PLANE zooms past the
camera, heading down. We track it and see it's falling out of
the sky!

INT. PLANE - CONTINUOUS

Pilot DANIEL JACKSON, 40s, absolutely focused, holds his
headset in place.

                    DANIEL
          Mayday, mayday, this is Echo 10-4!
          I've lost control of my plane!

EXT. SKY - CONTINUOUS

The plane plummets toward the Earth and crashes into the
ocean!

EXT. OCEAN - CONTINUOUS

The hollow remains of flight E10-4 slowly sink into the
depths of the sea.

TITLE CARD: "THE WRECK OF ECHO 10-4"

Chase music builds to a swell.

EXT. NEIGHBORHOOD - NIGHT

TIRES SCREECHING; POLICE SIRENS; LIGHTS FLASHING.

TRE, 18, in a dead sprint. He darts for a house, jumping the
fence.

EXT. BACKYARD - NIGHT

An OLDER COUPLE sit on their porch, staring.

                    TRE
          Oh... hey, Mr. Mills. Mrs. Mills.

POLICE surround him. Tre exhales in defeat.

TITLE CARD: "TRE"

THE SHOOTING SCRIPT

INT. JAIL - CELL - NIGHT

Tre sits in his cell, reading his bible.

JAILBIRD 1 passes by his cell.

                    INMATE 1
          Hey Tre.

                    TRE
          Hey Johnny.

JAILBIRD 2 passes by his cell.

                    INMATE 2
          What-up Tre?

                    TRE
          Richie, what's good?

OFFICER BURKE approaches Tre's cell.

                    TRE (CONT'D)
          Hey Burke, what's with the new
          cell?

                    BURKE
          Old one's not available...

Tre flinches. What could have happened in there?

                    BURKE (CONT'D)
          Nothing bad. Renovating. You ready
          for your phone call?

INT. JAIL - VISITOR BOOTH - NIGHT

Hazel, Tre's sister, sits across from him.

                    HAZEL
          What'd you do?

                    TRE
          Nothing this time. I swear.

                    HAZEL
          I told you, hang with the wrong
          people, you're gonna get blamed for
          stuff you didn't do.

                    TRE
          Sis, I ditched those guys.

                    HAZEL
          Then what? Are you stealing again?

                    TRE
          No. I honestly got no idea why I'm
          here.

Hazel breaks eye contact with Tre.

                    TRE (CONT'D)
          Don't tell Ms. Joy about this.

Hazel smiles.

                    HAZEL
          You better get out soon. You miss
          her birthday and--

                    TRE
          --"and I'll sleep on the porch."

                    BURKE
          2 minutes!

                    HAZEL
          I know we've got it rough. But this
          doesn't have to be our road. We can
          be different than dad.

Tre looks at her in disbelief.

                    TRE
          Yeah, maybe.

                    HAZEL
          Hey, before I go... your pilot
          friend. Name was Jackson, right?

                    TRE
          What's up?

Hazel breathes in, ready to break the news.

INT. INTERROGATION ROOM - DAY

Tre sits at a pale white table across from DETECTIVE MARCUS
BJORNSON, 40s, who eyes Tre intensely.

                    MARCUS
          So, Mr. Tracy Freeman--

                    TRE
          --Tre.

                    MARCUS
          Tre... What exactly was your
          relationship to Daniel Jackson?

                    TRE
          Met him a few years back.

INT. AIRPORT - DAY

Tre and Hazel stand at a grand airport window, looking out on
the runway. Daniel Jackson enters the frame, holding a
doughnut, talking on his cell.

                    DANIEL
          Cause you're out of control! How
          did you spend nine-hundred dollars
          on lunch? That's more than my jet
          fuel!

Daniel exits. Hazel smirks at Tre.

                    HAZEL
          Watch my stuff.

Tre nods as Hazel takes out her wallet and walks off.

Tre looks out the window at the runway as planes land. His
eyes fill with wonder.

Daniel Jackson still paces nearby with his phone to his ear.

His eyes hold on Tre, who is mesmerized by the planes. Dan
knowingly smiles. He sees himself in Tre.

The sound of his wife's BICKERING through the phone snaps him
back to reality.

                    STELLA (V.O.)
          You're selfish. You never think
          about anyone but yourself!

                    DANIEL
                (to himself)
          Selfish, huh?

He eyes Tre again.

                    DANIEL (CONT'D)
                (to Stella)
          You wouldn't think so if you had a
          job, instead of sitting home all
          day, spending my money.

Click. He hangs up.

Dan stuffs the last bite of the doughnut into his mouth and approaches Tre.

> DANIEL (CONT'D)
> Pretty amazing, isn't it?

> TRE
> It's alright.

Tre walks away, puts earbuds in, and sits down. Dan thinks better of it. Whatever. But his phone buzzes:

INSERT - PHONE

iMessage from Stella: "SELFISH!"

BACK TO SCENE.

Dan follows after Tre.

> DANIEL
> Is this seat taken?

Tre takes out his earbuds, looks up and around at all the other empty seats. He sighs.

> TRE
> All yours.

Dan sits down across from Tre.

> DANIEL
> (super friendly)
> So, where you headed?

> TRE
> (super deadpan)
> Dad's funeral.

> DANIEL
> Oh. Sorry to hear that.

> TRE
> Yeah, well he ran with the wrong
> crowd.

There's an awkward silence. Tre deliberates. Almost out of guilt, he engages:

> TRE (CONT'D)
> Where are you going?

                    DANIEL
          Flying to New York, but I'll be
          back later tonight.

Dan coyly points to his badge.

                    DANIEL (CONT'D)
          Pilot.

                    TRE
          That a cool job?

                    DANIEL
          Oh yeah.

                    TRE
          Always wanted to try it out.

                    DANIEL
          You want some lessons?

                    TRE
          Does it look like I got money?

                    DANIEL
          It's on the house.

                    TRE
          You're playing.

                    DANIEL
          I'm serious. I always wished
          someone would've done that for me.

Tre's shocked by his luck.

                    TRE
          Gee, thanks uh, mister...

                    DANIEL
          Just Dan. Dan Jackson.

                    TRE
          Tre. You doing this for me--that's
          very, uh...

                    DANIEL
          Selfless?

                    TRE
          Yeah.

                    DANIEL
          Tell that to my wife!

The two laugh. Beat.

                    DANIEL (CONT'D)
          Seriously, though.

EXT. SKY - DAY

Dan's plane drifts across the baby-blue sky.

INT. PLANE - DAY

Tre grips the controls with a wondrous, childlike smile.

Dan sits beside him, beaming with excitement.

                    DANIEL
          Feels like Soarin' at Epcot, right?

                    TRE
          Huh?

                    DANIEL
          Never mind. You're doing great kid!

EXT. SKY - DAY

The plane continues floating above the clouds.

                    TRE (V.O.)
          This is amazing.

                    DANIEL (V.O.)
          Makes you feel alive.

INT. INTERROGATION ROOM - DAY

                    MARCUS
          You're aware Dan Jackson died
          yesterday in a plane crash?

                    TRE
          Yeah. What's that got to do with
          me?

Marcus studies Tre.

                    MARCUS
          We recovered the plane and found
          that someone tampered with the oil
          compressor.
                    (MORE)

                    MARCUS (CONT'D)
          The plane was sabotaged. Dan
          Jackson was murdered.

Tre holds a stern gaze at Marcus, but a hint of surprise
glistens in his eyes.

                    MARCUS (CONT'D)
          And you're a suspect.

                    TRE
          Wait--what? Me? Why?

Marcus gives Tre a knowing look.

                    TRE (CONT'D)
          Look, it's just me, my sis, and Ms.
          Joy. But Mr. Jackson gave me a
          chance. He was teaching me how to
          fly. Why would I kill him?

                    MARCUS
          Cash. When did you learn about his
          will?

CLOSE ON Tre.

                                        MATCH CUT TO:

INT. COURTROOM - DAY

Tre, sitting at the witness stand.

                    TRE
          His will?

                    NOBLE
          His will.

The prosecutor, DENNIS NOBLE, eyes Tre suspiciously, then
sifts through his notes.

                    NOBLE (CONT'D)
          Mr. Jackson made an addendum on
          June 1st.

INT. DAN'S MANSION - KITCHEN - NIGHT

Dan and Tre laugh as they watch footage of their day's flight
training.

STELLA, Dan's wife, enters. She holds a piece of paper.
Seeing Tre, she sighs.

                    STELLA
          Hey boys--

                    DANIEL
          Stel' you gotta see this. I put a
          GoPro on the plane. Look at Tre's
          face!

                    STELLA
          Funny. Dan, can we speak about
          this?

She holds up the paper. Dan's smile fades.

                    DANIEL
          One sec, Tre.

Dan and Stella step a few paces from Tre and speak in a
hushed tone.

Tre politely scrubs through the footage, trying to appear
distracted. But as Dan and Stella's dialogue turns into an
argument, he hears:

                    STELLA
               (hushed)
          You won't give me a dime, but you
          wanna give him a quarter-million!?

                    DANIEL
          I thought you wanted me to be less
          selfish.

Stella crumples the paper and throws it in the trash,
storming out.

                    DANIEL (CONT'D)
          Stel! Honey...

Dan rushes after Stella.

Tre's alone. He deliberates for a beat. Then he silently
stands and creeps toward the garbage. He cranes his neck to
see down the hall. Nothing.

He surfs through the trash, finds the paper, and unwraps it.

INSERT - DAN'S WILL

TRACY FREEMAN. PLANE & $250,000.00

BACK TO SCENE.

Tre doubts. He reads it again. Then he jumps, smiles, emotes, but all quiet as a mouse. Then a sinister thought crosses his mind. A dark cloud sits over him.

A door opens and closes nearby, but out of sight. Tre folds the paper and slides it in his pocket.

INT. COURTROOM - DAY

Noble plays to the JURY.

                    NOBLE
          Two-hundred fifty thousand dollars.
          He writes you into his will and
          three days later, he's dead.
          Strange, right?

                    TRE
          Yeah.

                    NOBLE
          You learned you were added to the
          will prior to his death, correct?

Tre thinks hard before answering.

                    TRE
               (lying)
          This 'will' stuff is news to me.
          Never heard anything about a will.

Noble ponders. Switching gears.

                    NOBLE
          Says here you earned your private
          pilot's license on June 2nd, that
          correct?

                    TRE
          Yes.

                    NOBLE
          And you were hesitant to fly that
          day, isn't that so?

EXT. HANGAR - DAY

Dan's hangar sits on a grassy, private runway sitting just behind his home.

Tre kneels beside Dan's plane, working with a wrench. Two SHADOWS linger near him. He looks up and stands.

He scratches his chin, deliberating. Then he reaches off
screen to shake hands with one of the unidentified
characters.

                    TRE
          Deal.

INT. HANGAR - DAY

Dan is speaking with MRS. AVEL as Tre approaches.

                    DANIEL
          Great! Tre, this is Mrs. Avel. She
          will be conducting your flight test
          today.

                    AVEL
          A kid?

Tre gulps.

                    TRE
          Flight test?

                    AVEL
          You're going soft on me, Dan.

                    DANIEL
          That's an understatement. He's from
          Mangrove.

                    AVEL
          So you're a foster dad, too?

Tre exhales, stressed.

                    DANIEL
          C'mon Tre, you're more than ready.

Tre's visibly uncomfortable.

                    DANIEL (CONT'D)
              (to Avel)
          Give us a minute.

Dan walks with Tre, away from the plane.

                    DANIEL (CONT'D)
          What's going on? You love flying,
          don't you?

                    TRE
          Yeah.

DANIEL
It's no different than any other
flight.

Tre doesn't answer. But he sees Dan waiting, so he blurts
something out:

TRE
Something'll go wrong. Something
always does.

DANIEL
Don't be so dramatic, Tre.

TRE
Easy for you to say.

DANIEL
Tre, you got a good attitude and a
good work ethic. And that's a
choice you've made every day you
walked in this hangar. We got to
this point together. Now you choose
how far you can go.

INT. COCKPIT - DAY

Tre sits in the pilot's seat next to Avel, both wearing
headsets. Tre hesitates.

AVEL
You sure you're up for this, kid?
Wasn't planning on dying on the job
today.

Tre breathes. He eyes both propellers.

TRE
(cocky)
I'm good. Piece of cake.

Tre flicks switches and pulls the mic closer to his mouth.

TRE (CONT'D)
Ready for takeoff.

EXT. RUNWAY - DAY

The plane sits on the runway and begins to move forward.

INT. COCKPIT - DAY

Tre pushes the throttle forward. His eyes are locked, more
determined than ever before.

EXT. RUNWAY - DAY

The plane accelerates, shooting across the runway and up into
the air.

INT. COCKPIT - DAY

Tre pulls on the yoke as his body pushes back into his seat.
Mrs. Avel looks impressed and pleased.

EXT. HANGAR - DAY

Dan watches from the hangar as the plane flies into the air.
He cheers and smiles watching it soar.

INT. COCKPIT - DAY

Tre brings the plane to its proper elevation and lets the
plane cruise for a while. Avel looks down at her clipboard.

> AVEL
> Gotta say, I'm impressed. Never
> seen a kid from your side of town
> do anything like this.

Tre holds his gaze. Gee, thanks.

EXT. TRE'S HOUSE - NIGHT (FLASHBACK)

Red and blue lights flash behind TRE'S FATHER as he's
handcuffed by two COPS.

YOUNG TRE and YOUNG HAZEL, 5-10, watch from the stoop.

> COP 1
> Never a dull moment.

> COP 2
> What'd you expect? Mangrove's a
> dump.

Tre's neighbor, STEPHANIE JOY, comes out of her home and
watches the event in horror. She approaches Tre and takes his
hand.

                    JOY
          C'mon you two. You come with me
          now.

BEEP, BEEP...

INT. COCKPIT - BACK TO PRESENT

... BEEP, BEEP, BEEP. Tre snaps out of it. The plane is
turning to the side.

EXT. PLANE - DAY

One of the plane's engines is smoking!

INT. COCKPIT - DAY

Suddenly, the door cracks open a few inches. Air is sucked
out of the plane like a vacuum.

Tre grips the yoke tightly and pulls it in the opposite
direction.

                    TRE
          What do I do!?

No response. Avel has passed out. Tre notices the cracked
door.

INSERT - PRESSURE GAUGE

The cabin is losing pressure.

BACK TO SCENE.

Tre's face turns pale with fear. He grips the yoke, holding
the plane stable.

Eyeing the cracked door again, Tre violently throws the plane
left and right, trying to slam the door shut. It doesn't
budge.

In a last ditch effort, he unbuckles his seat belt and rushes
to the door, grabbing and heaving with all his might, pulling
the door shut.

Tre dives back over to his seat and grabs the yoke, yanking
it back to stabilize the plane.

Tre grabs his headset and puts it back on. He flicks a
switch.

                    TRE (CONT'D)
               (out of breath)
          Tracy Freeman, Echo 10-4, emergency
          landing!

Tre clamps his hands around the yoke.

INT. COCKPIT - DAY

Tre's fear is gone. Now it's pain and determination. He
pushes forward on the yoke and begins to descend.

EXT. PLANE - DAY

The plane descends from the sky and is heading steadily to
safety.

EXT. HANGAR - DAY

Dan nervously watches as the plane descends.

                    DANIEL
          Come on, Tre.

INT. COCKPIT - DAY

Tre pulls on the yoke, slowing down to prepare for the
landing. He flicks a switch.

EXT. PLANE - DAY

The wheels of the plane come out. The plane hits the ground
and shoots across the runway.

EXT. HANGAR - DAY

Dan lets out a sigh of relief.

                    DANIEL
          Way to go, kid.

INT. COCKPIT - DAY

Tre pulls the plane to a stop. He lets out a sigh and a smile
emerges on his face. It fades as he quickly turns to Mrs.
Avel.

INT. HANGAR - LATER

Mrs. Avel is no longer unconscious. She sits in a chair along
with Dan and Tre who are both concerned for her.

                    DANIEL
               (to Avel)
          So... how'd he do?

Avel stands to pace away, and is followed by Daniel.

                    AVEL
          I don't know. I wasn't conscious!
          Those are serious issues with your
          plane--

                    DANIEL
          --I take full responsibility for
          them.

                    AVEL
          Who else should?

                    DANIEL
          But don't take it out on the kid.
          He's--

                    AVEL
          Are you kidding? I wouldn't be
          alive if it wasn't for him.

Tre butts-in to the conversation.

                    TRE
          Yeah, yeah I saved your life. No
          big deal, but did I pass?

Avel nods. Tre's face lights up! He embraces Dan.

                    AVEL
          Get that plane checked-out, Dan.
          Today.

                    DANIEL
          Will do!

Avel exits.

                    AVEL (O.S.)
          Unbelievable!

17

INT. COURTROOM - DAY

                    NOBLE
          There was an issue with the plane?

                    TRE
          The starboard engine overheated.
          Started smoking.

                    NOBLE
          Mrs. Avel testified you were
          hesitant to get on the plane. She
          heard you say, "Something'll go
          wrong."

Tre realizes what's going on.

                    TRE
          Yeah I was nervous. But not cause I
          sabotaged the plane or something.

                    NOBLE
          I didn't say you sabotaged the
          plane.

                    TRE
          No, I see what you're doing. How
          stupid would I have to be to get in
          a plane knowing it had a broken
          propeller?

                    NOBLE
          You knew the issue ahead of time,
          so you knew how to fly and correct
          it.

                    TRE
          Sure, but why would I risk wrecking
          a plane that I'm supposed to
          inherit?

                    NOBLE
          So you knew about the will?!

                    TRE
          Uh... no. I'm saying...

Noble looks to the JURORS, who stare intently at Tre.

                    TRE (CONT'D)
          If I knew about the will--like you
          were arguing.

                    NOBLE
          Don't play stupid, Tracy. You know
          that wasn't Dan's only plane.

Noble takes beat to adjust his approach.

                    NOBLE (CONT'D)
          Where were you on June 8th...

INT. INTERROGATION ROOM - DAY

                    MARCUS
          ... The day of the wreck. Don't
          leave anything out.

Tre thinks long and hard. He breathes in, then out.

                    TRE
          I went to Mr. Jackson's house.

EXT. DAN'S MANSION - DAY

                    TRE (V.O.)
          Wanted to invite him to dinner with
          me, Hazel, and Ms. Joy. Thank him
          for all he'd done.

Tre approaches the door and is surprised to find it ever-so-
slightly ajar.

INT. DAN'S MANSION - ENTRANCE - DAY

Tre opens cautiously and enters.

                    TRE (V.O.)
          It was weird. Door was open. And he
          and his wife were fighting again.

Stella immediately storms past, tears in her eyes. Tre moves
in the opposite direction.

INT. DAN'S MANSION - OFFICE - DAY

Tre finds Daniel sitting alone.

                    TRE
          Everything alright Mr. Jackson?

> DANIEL
> (sarcastically)
> Living the dream. You got a girl,
> Tre?

> TRE (V.O.)
> But pretty soon, we hear something
> coming from the living room.

INT. INTERROGATION ROOM - DAY

> MARCUS
> What did you see?

> TRE
> A guy. A big guy.

Marcus' eyes squint and notes something down on his legal
pad.

> TRE (CONT'D)
> Mr. Jackson told me to run, so I
> ran!

EXT. DAN'S MANSION - YARD/AIRFIELD - DAY

Tre sprints away from the house.

> NOBLE (V.O.)
> So you ran all the way home?
> Without stopping anywhere?

Tre stops by the wall of the hangar. He sees GIUSEPPE, a
large Italian man, pursuing Dan out of the house.

> TRE (V.O.)
> (lying)
> Yeah. I ran straight home.

Tre runs up to an empty fuel pump, grabs the pump nozzle and
hose, and then runs off screen.

INT. COURTROOM - DAY

Tre looks off to Stephanie Joy, now his adoptive mother, in
the crowd. Noble paces slowly in front of Tre. The courtroom
is silent.

> NOBLE
> You returned home, but you didn't
> stay there.

                    TRE
          No. I get home...

INT. TRE'S HOUSE - EVENING

Tre enters his house. It's nothing grand. Tre looks big
inside it. He looks around to see if anyone is there.

                    TRE
          Ms. Joy? I'm home.

Joy rounds the corner.

                    JOY
          Did you invite him?

                    TRE
               (lying; guiltily)
          Oh... yeah. Said he'd love to.
          Tomorrow night.

                    JOY
          Good. You know, we have to
          celebrate. If only you had a mama
          who would have prepared. Oh that's
          right, you do. There's cake in the
          kitchen.

                    TRE
          And that's why you're the best!

                    JOY
          Don't forget it! You celebrating me
          next.

                    TRE
          Right, your birthday.

                    JOY
          You didn't forget, did you?

Tre shrugs cheekily.

                    JOY (CONT'D)
          Tracy Freeman, you forget my
          birthday and you'll sleep on the
          porch.

They laugh as they turn towards the kitchen.

INT. TRE'S HOUSE - NIGHT

Tre and Hazel enjoy a slice of cake, sitting on their couch.
The TV is on and playing in the background.

                    TV NEWS REPORTER
          Just over an hour ago, a plane
          crashed off the coast of Palm Beach
          Island. The cause of the crash is
          still unknown. The plane has been
          identified as Flight E10-4, a
          private jet owned and operated by
          local air force veteran...

Tre's smiles fades.

BANG, BANG, BANG. Someone's at the door.

                    JOY (O.S.)
          I'll get it, lazy bones.

She enters and heads towards the door. Tre gets up and moves
away from the front door.

                    HAZEL
          What are you doing?

EXT. TRE'S HOUSE - NIGHT

Joy opens the door. TWO COPS.

                    COP 1
          Good Evening, Ms. Joy.

                    JOY
          What'd he do this time?

                    COP 2
          We just wanna ask Tre a few
          questions, is all.

INT. TRE'S HOUSE - NIGHT

                    HAZEL
          Tre, don't!

Tre bolts out the back door of the house.

EXT. NEIGHBORHOOD - NIGHT

Tre darts down the street. He looks back and sees the police
stationed outside his house. Not looking, he trips on a
garbage can. BANG! The cops look towards the noise.

                    COP 1
          He's running!

TIRES SCREECHING; POLICE SIRENS; LIGHTS FLASHING.

Tre sprints away. He darts for a house, jumping the fence.

EXT. BACKYARD - NIGHT

An OLDER COUPLE sits on their porch, staring.

                    TRE
          Oh... hey, Mr. Mills. Mrs. Mills.

POLICE surround him. Tre exhales in defeat.

                    TRE (V.O.)
          They arrested me for no reason.

INT. COURTROOM - DAY

Noble paces as Tre finishes his story.

                    NOBLE
          They arrested you for running.

                    TRE
          Like I said, no reason.

                    NOBLE
          Innocent people don't run.

                    TRE
          It was out of habit, I guess. I'm
          not usually innocent.

Tre glances at Hazel in the crowd while Noble eyes the jury
with a smile.

Detective Bjornson sits in the gallery, watching intently.

                    TRE (CONT'D)
          A guy was chasing Mr. Jackson! The
          big guy. Why don't you talk to him?

                    NOBLE
          Thank you for your time, Mr.
          Freeman.

Tre returns from the witness stand to his seat. HOLD ON TRE.

                    NOBLE (CONT'D)
          The prosecution calls to the
          stand...

We glide past Tre, Ms. Joy, Hazel, and a few other bystanders
until we land on...

                    NOBLE (CONT'D)
          Stella Jackson.

INT. COURTROOM - DAY

Sweep across the courtroom AUDIENCE, featuring saddened and
empathetic faces, as we hear the painful sobs of STELLA
JACKSON, seated at the witness stand.

TRE FREEMAN cringes as he tries to understand her
incomprehensible blabber.

A stoic STENOGRAPHER. She hands a single tissue to JUDGE
BRICKMAN who gives it to the distraught Stella. She blows her
nose obnoxiously loud.

                    BRICKMAN
          Noble, please repeat the question
          to your witness.

NOBLE takes a conflicted sigh before addressing Stella.

                    NOBLE
          Mrs. Jackson, you described your
          relationship with the deceased as--

                    STELLA
          You mean my husband, tonto!

                    NOBLE
          I apologize Mrs. Jackson. You
          described your husband as--

                    STELLA
          He was the love of my life, and I
          was the moon in his sky. There was
          nothing else I needed. But then
          he...

GIUSEPPE L'AQUILA is escorted into the courtroom and catches
Stella off-guard. He takes a seat.

                    STELLA (CONT'D)
               (through conjured tears)
          ... died! And I'll never get to see
          him again!

                    NOBLE
          I understand, Mrs. Jackson--

                    STELLA
          We had everything, and I loved him!

                    NOBLE
          Mrs. Jackson--

                    STELLA
          And now he's... he's gone!

Judge Brickman bangs his gavel three times.

                    BRICKMAN
          Mr. Noble, let's allow Mrs. Jackson
          to collect herself. We'll reconvene
          after a short recess.
               (to himself)
          I need an aspirin.

TITLE CARD: STELLA

INT. COURT HALLWAY - DAY

Stella closes the court door behind her and rubs her eyes.
She's completely fine and proud of her heart-wrenching act.

She waits down the hall, watching the doors to the courtroom.
Giuseppe exits and sees Stella.

Stella turns the corner stealthily, waiting for him. Giuseppe
joins her.

                    STELLA
               (hushed)
          What are you doing here?

Stella makes sure they are truly alone.

                    GIUSEPPE
          You tell me.

                    STELLA
          Don't be stupid, I'm not a rat.

                    GIUSEPPE
          The kid must've said something.

                    STELLA
          He did. He mentioned a "big guy."

                    GIUSEPPE
          Well, he got that right.

                    STELLA
          Just keep your mouth shut in there.
          You could ruin everything.

                    GIUSEPPE
          I could ruin you.

                    STELLA
               (threateningly)
          If you talk, I talk. Got it?

Giuseppe smirks. He likes this girl.

INT. COURTROOM - DAY

Stella stands at the witness stand. She starts to take her
seat...

                                        MATCH CUT TO:

INT. INTERROGATION ROOM - DAY

Stella finishes taking her seat.

                    STELLA
          Nice to see you again.

                    MARCUS
          Likewise.

                    STELLA
          Why am I here?

                    MARCUS
          Mrs. Jackson, I understand your
          relationship with Daniel was
          strained.

                    STELLA
          How did you know that?

                    MARCUS
          A source.
               (empathetic)
          Listen, I know all about your
          situation. The break-in? I want to
          help. Just tell me the truth.

Stella's unsure. Marcus clicks his pen to his legal pad.

                    MARCUS (CONT'D)
          So you and your husband. Can you
          elaborate?

INT. DAN'S MANSION - ENTRANCE - NIGHT

Dan enters the house and is embraced by Stella. She's hugging
him a little too hard.

                    DANIEL
          I missed you too, Stel.

                    STELLA
          It's so late. What happened?

Stella is clingy and nosy. Even this early in their marriage,
Dan's a bit tired of her.

Dan takes off his coat and puts down his bag.

                    DANIEL
          Sorry, babe. New client, more
          flights, but it's fine now. I'm
          home.

Dan walks over and gently kisses Stella's forehead, which
appeases her. For a moment.

                    STELLA
          Okay, but this has been going on a
          lot and--

                    DANIEL
          I know, Stel. I promise it won't
          happen again.

Stella takes a deep breath.

                    STELLA
          Alright. Well, let me heat up
          dinner. It's Pasta Alla Vodka!

INT. DAN'S MANSION - LIVING ROOM - NIGHT

Adjacent to the entrance foyer.

Dan and Stella, sitting on the couch, enjoy their meal and good conversation.

                                        MATCH CUT TO:

INT. DAN'S MANSION - LIVING ROOM - A FEW NIGHTS LATER

Stella sits alone with a sour look on her face, holding a glass of wine. Keys jingle and the door opens from behind her. Dan enters.

                    STELLA
          Again.

                    DANIEL
          I know, I know, babe, I just had to
          do a flight--

                    STELLA
          --for the new client. I know.

Dan walks around the couch and gently kisses Stella's forehead. Stella's face remains tense and stoic.

                    DANIEL
          Where'd you get this?

Dan gestures to Stella's pearl necklace.

                    STELLA
          A store.

                    DANIEL
          How much did it cost?

                    STELLA
              (cheeky)
          Nada.

                    DANIEL
              (appalled)
          You stole it?!

Stella takes a sip of her wine. Daniel's about to lose it but calms himself down.

                    DANIEL (CONT'D)
          Why?

                    STELLA
          It's fun.

She's enjoying the attention.

                    DANIEL
          I don't care how much it costs--I'd
          rather you pay for it.

                    STELLA
              (mischievous)
          If you say so.

INT. DAN'S MANSION - LIVING ROOM - MONTAGE

-Two dishes sit on the coffee table. Stella reads a book and
waits for Dan, occasionally eyeing the door and clock.

-Two dishes sit on the coffee table. Stella's in her PJs
watching TV. She looks to the door, waiting... waiting.

-Stella holds a glass of white wine with no food, waiting for
Dan.

-In different PJs, Stella's asleep on the couch.

-An empty living room.

INT. INTERROGATION ROOM - DAY

                    STELLA
          I barely saw him, but we still
          talked every day.

                    MARCUS
          And those talks were cordial?

                    STELLA
          Of course!

INT. RENATA'S RISTORANTE - DAY

                    STELLA
          What is wrong with you?

With her phone to her ear, Stella paces across Renata's
Ristorante, bumping into Giuseppe momentarily (who she hasn't
met yet).

                    DANIEL (V.O.)
          What?

                    STELLA
          You froze my credit card!

                    DANIEL (V.O.)
          Cause you're out of control! How
          did you spend nine-hundred dollars
          on lunch? That's more than my jet
          fuel!

                    STELLA
          I'm out with Dee right now and I
          told her I'd pay!

She eyes Diane who's sitting across the room, oblivious.

                    DANIEL (V.O.)
          How bout she spends her husband's
          money for a change.

The shame! The embarrassment! The humanity!

                    STELLA
          You're selfish. You never think
          about anyone but yourself!

                    DANIEL (V.O.)
          You wouldn't think so if you had a
          job, instead of sitting home all
          day spending my money.

Click. Stella looks at her phone in disbelief. Did he just
hang up on me?!

She ponders a moment. Her face reads "challenge accepted."

INT. CAFE - DAY

A LONG LINE of ANGRY CUSTOMERS. Stella comes face to face
with a complicated espresso machine.

Tre walks in the cafe peering at the crowded line and waves
to HAZEL who works alongside Stella. Tre and Stella make eye
contact.

Stella's head grows hot. The toaster oven BEEPS; Stella drops
a hot pastry, picks it up, and gives it to the customer; she
frantically tries to use the milk frother until what's left
of the milk violently explodes in her face. Tre feels bad for
her.

The LEAD BARISTA, covered in milk, fuming with anger, points
Stella to the door.

THE SHOOTING SCRIPT

EXT. CAFE - DAY

Stella sits outside on a lonely curb defeated. Dan was right.
She tries to comb out the milk residue in her hair. Tre walks
out the door to Stella. She notices him and tries to make
herself look halfway decent. Tre awkwardly stands next to
Stella. They both dread the dead silence.

                    STELLA
          Line's probably a lot shorter now
          if you want to order something.

                    TRE
          No, yeah, I just uh... wanted to
          see if everything was alright.

                    STELLA
          Yes, Tracy. I'm fine. I don't need
          your sympathy.

                    TRE
          No disrespect Mrs. Jackson. I was--

                    STELLA
          What else am I supposed to do? Dan
          cut me off, and I'm not good at
          anything.

She's on the verge of tears. Tre takes a seat beside her.

                    TRE
          For what it's worth, I think you're
          doing great.

Stella looks at him with eyes that read: "Really?"

                    TRE (CONT'D)
          Last year I was outta cash. Me and
          my buddies swiped a few things from
          drugstores and pawned 'em off. Sent
          me to juvi.

                    STELLA
          Okay, Tracy, and your point?

                    TRE
          You're working hard. Trying to do
          things the right way.

                    STELLA
          You sound like my husband.

                    TRE
          Yeah, is that bad?

                    STELLA
          Hate to burst your bubble, but he's
          not like us. He was born rich and
          he'll die rich.

                    TRE
          And?

                    STELLA
          So who is he to tell us how to
          struggle?

INT. INTERROGATION ROOM - DAY

                    STELLA
          Butcher, construction worker,
          barista... it was awful.

                    MARCUS
               (sarcastic)
          You poor thing.

                    STELLA
          And that wasn't the worst of it.

EXT. GT ELEMENTARY SCHOOL - DAY

Stella stares at the building -- Giacomo Tanti Elementary
School. She's hit rock bottom. A school. With children.

                    PRINCIPAL (V.O.)
          Mrs. Jackson, may I ask why you
          left your previous job?

INT. PRINCIPAL'S OFFICES - DAY

Stella sits in her black Gucci pencil skirt and her pink
Valentino top in a crusty principal's office. She's repulsed
by everything in sight.

                    STELLA
          I'm lactose intolerant. The milk
          wasn't good for me.

                    PRINCIPAL
          Alright... So, it says on your
          resume that you have a degree in
          finance?

                    STELLA
          That's right.

PRINCIPAL
But you have no other prolonged
work experience?

STELLA
I was a receptionist for a year.

PRINCIPAL
Exciting.

Stella's smile drops.

PRINCIPAL (CONT'D)
So, why do you want to work at this
school?

STELLA
I love children.

The Principal is not buying it

PRINCIPAL
Mrs. Jackson, I want to remind you
that our faculty takes the
conditions of our students and
environment very seriously.

Stella looks around.

STELLA
I bet you do.

PRINCIPAL
You applied for 'Future Staff
Openings'. Are you willing to take
our first available opening, no
matter the position?

STELLA
Of course!

INT. SCHOOL HALLWAY - DAY

Stella slops a wet mop on the dirty hallway floor,
lethargically swishing and swashing in one place.

EXT. GT ELEMENTARY SCHOOL - DAY

Stella wipes down the muddy tires of a school bus. The BUS
LADY sits on a down-turned bucket and watches Stella work.

                    BUS LADY
          Been wanting to take better care of
          these babies. May not look like
          much, but you're scrubbing a
          hundred-thousand dollar investment.

                    STELLA
               (under breath)
          For a hundred grand this thing
          should clean itself.

                    BUS LADY
          You missed a spot.

The Bus Lady points from her bucket throne. Stella grits her
teeth and wipes the tire faster.

EXT. GT ELEMENTARY SCHOOL - BREEZEWAY - DAY

Muddy and disheveled, Stella takes her dirty rags to a
trashcan when a miserable-looking BALLET TEACHER throws her
half-filled cup of coffee in the trash, splattering it on
Stella.

Stella furrows her brows and grips her mop, contemplating
whether hitting the teacher is worth the jail time. ANGELINA,
5-6 year old student with a hall pass and used tissue,
strolls by.

                    STELLA
          Psst! Hey!

The child looks in her direction cautiously.

                    STELLA (CONT'D)
               (whispering)
          Come here.

The little girl walks toward her, and Stella leans in.

                    STELLA (CONT'D)
          Hey, where's that teacher's room?

The little girl points behind Stella down the hall looking in
the direction of her small hand. Suddenly Angelina sneezes on
Stella.

Stella struggles to breathe. Apologetically, the child hands
her the used tissue.

INT. BALLET STUDIO - DAY

Stella enters the empty studio, tugging her janitor cart
along. She tip-toes to the teacher's desk. She takes picture
frames off the desk and smashes them! She rips up paper and
flings a binder across the room. Her sinister smile fades as
she holds up a shiny laptop.

She pulls out a garbage bag from her janitor cart and stuffs
the laptop inside. She thinks for a moment--debating her
actions. Then she gives in:

She proceeds to stuff cash, jewelry, and more into her
garbage bag.

On her way out, she sees a rack of beautiful golden dresses;
show costumes. She adds a few to her sack and makes out like
the Grinch.

                    NOBLE (V.O.)
          Mrs. Jackson, going back to work
          wasn't easy, now was it?

INT. COURTROOM - DAY

Stella sits at the witness stand all pretty and postured.
Dennis Noble eyes her, standing before her.

                    STELLA
          No, not exactly.

                    NOBLE
          Did cutting you off from your
          entitled resources spawn any
          hateful intentions toward your
          husband?

                    STELLA
          Excuse me?

                    NOBLE
          According to the bank statements,
          Mr. Jackson didn't just freeze you
          out of one credit card account, but
          all four, in addition to your main
          joint account. Now... would you say
          he went too far? Excessive maybe?

                    STELLA
          Yes, I believe it was excessive.

                    NOBLE
          Mrs. Jackson, your husband told you
          about the change to his will,
          adding Tracy Freeman as a
          benefactor of a plane and $250,000
          dollars?

                    STELLA
               (lying)
          Of course! He wouldn't hide
          something like that from me.

                    NOBLE
          He cuts you off but grants Mr.
          Freeman a quarter million
          inheritance. Did that upset you?

Her defense attorney, JULIANNA, suddenly stands up.

                    JULIANNA
          Objection! Leading the witness.

                    BRICKMAN
          Overruled.

                    STELLA
          I was proud of him for being so
          selfless.

The jury whisper to one another. Tre fumes with anger.

INT. RENATA'S RISTORANTE - DAY

An empty wine bottle slams on the table. Diane releases the
bottle and leans back.

                    DIANE
          Congrats, Stel. Three days is your
          longest one yet. I'm so proud of
          you, girl.

                    STELLA
          I'll be proud when all of this crap
          is over.

                    DIANE
          I don't care if I was dirt poor, I
          would never work at a school. It's
          filthy.

GIO, a cocky and smart booty kid, approaches the table.

                    GIO
          Excuse me. Your check, ma'am.

                    STELLA
          Hold on.

Stella unfolds four $50 bills from her pink purse and hands
it to Gio as he counts it and smiles. He steps in closer.

                    GIO
          Your tip, ma'am?

Stella stares at Gio and looks hard. Finally, she pulls out
one more fifty before placing the cash in his hand. Gio
almost bolts out of sight before a second thought can come to
mind.

Diane looks at Stella in shock.

                    DIANE
          Um. Stella, sweetheart, you want to
          explain where you got that cash?

                    STELLA
          Dan is making me revert to... other
          lucrative habits.

                    DIANE
          Stella!

                    STELLA
          Oh, not like that, Dee.

She takes a small beat as she looks around.

                    STELLA (CONT'D)
              (softly)
          I just took a few things from the
          school and pawned them off.

                    DIANE
          You stole!?

                    STELLA
          Sh! Could you say that any louder?

Diane leans back with a wicked smirk, totally impressed. The
gall. The mischief!

                    DIANE
          I've always wanted to try that. But
          I wouldn't know where to start.

                    STELLA
          I think I know a guy.

EXT. AIRFIELD - DAY

Tre works meticulously greasing a pile of gear wheel
bearings. He sees shadows creep up behind him. Tre turns
around quickly to reveal a not-so-threatening Stella and
Diane in their black Gucci high heels.

                    TRE
          Oh! Hi, Mrs. Jackson. And, uh, nice
          to meet you...

Tre stands and stretches out his hand for Diane to shake it.
She almost does, but notices his oily, black-stained palms.

                    DIANE
          Eww.

She withdraws her hands as Stella peels off her black
sunglasses.

                    STELLA
          My sweet Tracy. We need your
          particular assistance.

                    TRE
          With?

                    DIANE
          Stealing.

                    TRE
          Wait-what? Stealing! Mrs. Jackson
          what happened to putting in the
          work?

                    STELLA
          I tried it. Didn't go so well.

                    TRE
          Well I gave that stuff up. And I
          really can't afford another charge.

                    DIANE
          What do you want? Money? We've got
          it.

                    STELLA
              (quietly)
          No, we don't.

Tre eyes catch on a glimmer of light shining from Stella's
pure white pearl necklace. Light bulb. A tainted light bulb.

> TRE
> That's a nice necklace you got
> there, Mrs. Jackson.

He points to the necklace.

> TRE (CONT'D)
> It'd look pretty good on Ms. Joy.
> Her birthday is coming up.

> STELLA
> Are you kidding? Absolutely not.

> TRE
> Fine by me.

Tre moves to continue his task. The opportunity is slipping.
Diane shoots an impatient look at Stella. Stella rolls her
eyes and takes off the necklace and offers it out to Tre.

> STELLA
> Fine! Deal?

Tre deliberates.

> TRE
> Deal.

They shake hands and seal the deal. Stella looks at her now
black hands.

> STELLA
> Eww.

INT. COURTROOM - DAY

Stella stares at Noble as she sits in the stand.

> NOBLE
> So, Mrs. Jackson, how did you fare
> living without your normal income?

> STELLA
> I managed. I learned how to get by
> with the little I had. It worked
> out.

                    NOBLE
          Mrs. Jackson, did your husband have
          any enemies? Anyone who would have
          wanted to hurt him?

Stella looks to Giuseppe who returns her stoic gaze.

INT. DAN'S MANSION - LIVING ROOM - DAY

Shattered glass, broken lamps, an eerie feeling lurks in the
air. A frightened Stella wraps a protective silk blanket
around herself as she comically grips a butter knife in her
hand, backing towards the corner.

INT. DAN'S MANSION - LIVING ROOM - MOMENTS LATER

Stella's on the phone with Dan, sitting on the floor

                    STELLA
          I WAS HOME ALONE! Someone broke in
          and I was ALONE!

                    DANIEL (V.O.)
          What do you want from me?

                    STELLA
          I'm scared, Dan. Where are you?

                    DANIEL (V.O.)
          Everything's fine, Stel.

                    STELLA
          I don't feel safe. You need to come
          home, that's what you need to do.

                    DANIEL (V.O.)
          I will. In a few weeks.

                    STELLA
          Weeks?!

                    GIUSEPPE (V.O.)
          Weeks?!

She looks at her phone, wondering if her mind played a trick
on her.

                    STELLA
          Dan...

                    DANIEL (V.O.)
          Just hire someone to stay at the
          house with you.

                    STELLA
               (sarcastic)
          Oh yeah. With all the money I have
          access to right now.

                    DANIEL
          Listen, I got to go. I'll call you
          in a bit.

The phone hangs up. Silence surrounds Stella.

A KNOCK pounds through the hollow house. Stella's eyes go
wide with terror.

INT. DAN'S MANSION - ENTRANCE - DAY

The door opens revealing DETECTIVE MARCUS BJORNSON. Stella,
still wearing her silk armor and butter knife sighs in
relief.

                    MARCUS
          Palm Beach Police.

EXT. DAN'S MANSION - LATER

Diane and Stella track with Marcus as he walks down the
driveway toward his car, finishing notes on his legal pad.

                    STELLA
          My husband thinks we should hire
          someone.

                    MARCUS
          Honestly, ma'am, that may be your
          best option.

                    STELLA
          Seriously?

                    MARCUS
          We've got nothing. Security cameras
          disabled, no witnesses... they knew
          what they were doing.

Stella eyes Marcus. Something feels familiar.

                    MARCUS (CONT'D)
          We'll keep an eye on your home but
          a security guard is a good
          precaution.

                    STELLA
          Have we met before? I know you from
          somewhere.

                    MARCUS
          Most likely. Been here a long time.
          Have a good day, Mrs. Jackson.

Marcus exits.

                    STELLA
               (sarcastic)
          Great. How many places do we need
          to rob to hire a bodyguard?

                    DIANE
          Jeanie's got one. Says she pays him
          a hundred grand a year.

That gives Stella an idea.

EXT. GT ELEMENTARY SCHOOL - NIGHT

Stella and Diane, dressed from head to toe in Gucci black,
sit lowly behind a bush outside the bus gate. Diane's purple
sparkly beanie sticks out like a sore thumb.

                    DIANE
          Ya know, Stel, There's a jeweler's
          down the road. They're still open.

                    STELLA
          Oh come on, Dee, it'll be easy.
          Security is a joke. We'll be in and
          out.

                    DIANE
          Okay... okay. Cameras?

                    STELLA
          I.T. guy quit before I did. Cameras
          are down. A third grader can rob
          this place.
               (to herself)
          I'm pretty sure one did...

                    DIANE
          So what are we waiting for?

                    STELLA
          Him.

An older man, SECURITY GUARD 1, with his keys jingling, walks
across the bus lot. Shifts are changing. He loads up in his
car and drives his out of the lot. The gate opens for him.

                    STELLA (CONT'D)
          Go!

Stella and Diane run up to the perimeter fence.

                    STELLA (CONT'D)
          Jump the fence.

                    DIANE
          I can't.

                    STELLA
          Why?

                    DIANE
          I'm in heels.

                    STELLA
          Diane!

A flashlight beams around the corner. Someone is coming. Time
is ticking.

                    STELLA (CONT'D)
          C'mon!

Stella and Diane rush to the bottom of the fence. They start
to scale. The light gets closer. Hearts beating.

THUD! The girls' feet reach the floor.

The flashlight shines along the fence. Site's clear. SECURITY
GUARD 2 enters his pin, and the gates open. He enters the lot
as Stella and Diane discreetly hide behind a bush.

Stella and Diane sneak as incognito as possible to a bus.
They are about to get to their getaway bus when a flashlight
almost detects them. SECURITY GUARD 3! A portly man.

They slither back to the shadows.

                    DIANE
          I thought you said this place had
          crap security.

                    STELLA
          They do. Did.

                    DIANE
          You distract that guard, I'll go
          get the bus.

The two split off in different directions.

Security Guard 2 walks around, staring off at the empty bus
lot. He hears a sound near one of the buses. Looking, he sees
a dark figure (Diane) moving at a distance. He goes to
investigate the motion.

Security Guard 2 shines his light where Diane just was.
Nothing.

INT. SCHOOL BUS - NIGHT

Reveal Diane in the bus, sighing in relief. The guard's
flashlight beams outside and slowly fades away.

Diane sits in the driver's seat, very confused. She looks
around, feeling for where the keys would be. Something shiny
catches her eye. There: The keys dangling on a little hook.

EXT. GT ELEMENTARY SCHOOL - NIGHT

Security Guard 3, a portly man, paces on the sidewalk.

Stella's quick but not quick enough before the guard shines
the light directly at her. Great. She runs. Guard 3 pursues,
but may have eaten one-too-many donuts.

                    SECURITY GUARD 3
          Hey! Get back here!

Stella runs, zig zagging through the maze of school buses.

                    SECURITY GUARD 3 (CONT'D)
          Tommy--over here!

Security Guard 2 joins the chase. Stella reaches a dead end.
Of course. She turns around as the guards finally catch up.
Guard 2 draws a handgun.

                    SECURITY GUARD 2
          Don't move! Stay right there.

A bright light blinds them as they see a BIG YELLOW SCHOOL
BUS heading right for them!

At the last second, both Guards leap for their lives, out of
the way. Security Guard 1's gun falls out of his clutch.

Stella rushes to pick it up and runs to the bus. Diane opens the door. Stella's about to step aboard when SOMETHING GRABS HER LEG! It's Security Guard 2, lying prone.

                    SECURITY GUARD 2 (CONT'D)
          Come here, you!

Stella turns around and punches him square in the face. He releases her.

                    STELLA
          Ow!

Her nail broke. She snatches his handgun off the ground.

INT./EXT. SCHOOL BUS - NIGHT

                    DIANE
          Come on, Stel. I'm on fire, baby!
          Let's ditch this-

                    STELLA
          Diane.

Stella hops on bus.

                    DIANE
          What?

                    STELLA
          You're amazing.

                    DIANE
          You, too, boo.

Diane closes the bus doors and starts to drive. She presses down on the gas, almost through the floor.

EXT. GT ELEMENTARY SCHOOL - NIGHT

The bus is going, going, going... and... BAM! The bus goes right through the gates. Stella and Diane are home free.

INT. SCHOOL BUS - NIGHT

                    DIANE
          You broke a nail?

                    STELLA
          Yeah, I'm fine.

                    DIANE
          You gotta learn how to punch.
          Kickboxing, karate, or something.

                    STELLA
          That'll be the day.

EXT. ROAD - NIGHT

The school bus drifts down a quiet, suburban road.

                    DIANE
          So how exactly are we supposed to
          sell this?

                    STELLA
          I'm not sure. We gotta hide it till
          we find a seller.

EXT. DAN'S MANSION - DAY

Everything looks normal except for the not-so-discreet big
yellow school bus hidden under a large tarp. A car pulls in.

INT. DAN'S MANSION - ENTRANCE - DAY

Stella and Diane almost run to the door.

Stella nervously shakes her hands, and the two ladies make
themselves presentable.

                    STELLA
          This is it. First Interview! Ready?

                    DIANE
          Wait! What am I supposed to do? I
          don't know what to do.

                    STELLA
          How should I know, Dee?

                    DIANE
          What do I say?

                    STELLA
          Nothing. Something. Just don't say
          anything stupid.

                    DIANE
          I'll try. What if he asks about the
          bus?

                    STELLA
          We change the topic.

Stella exhales as she opens the door for the big reveal. In
front of her stands the big, the strong, the handsome:
Giuseppe L'Aquila. Stella is in a trance.

                    NOBLE (V.O.)
          Mrs. Jackson...

INT. COURTROOM - DAY

Stella once again sits in the witness stand. All eyes are
daggered on her. She feels the slightest bit of pressure.

                    NOBLE
          The man you hired was Giuseppe
          L'Aquila?

                    STELLA
          Yes.

Shifting gears.

                    NOBLE
          Where were you on June 8th? The day
          of the incident?

                    STELLA
          I was at home. Dan had just come
          back for the first time in a few
          weeks. We were so happy and excited
          to be with each other again.

                    NOBLE
          Mr. Freeman testified you were
          fighting.

                    STELLA
          Well... we did have a minor
          argument. But all couples do.

INT. DAN'S MANSION - OFFICE - DAY

Stella throws a wine glass at Dan. It shatters on the wall
behind him.

                    STELLA (V.O.)
          We talked about our finances, but
          we handled it like adults.

                    NOBLE (V.O.)
          And what happened after that?

EXT. DAN'S MANSION - YARD/AIRFIELD - DAY

                    STELLA (V.O.)
          I went for a walk. I needed to calm
          my nerves a bit.

Stella arrives at the airfield and starts moving like she's
on a mission. Her face is hysterical and she's wielding a
pair of scissors.

She wrenches open a panel on the side of the plane! She puts
her scissors up to a line of cables. She debates. But then...

                    VOICE (O.S.)
               (distant)
          What are you doing?

INT. COURTROOM - DAY

                    STELLA
          I cooled down and went back to the
          house. I must've missed Dan on the
          way out. I never saw him again.

She eyes down Tre in the crowd.

                    STELLA (CONT'D)
          I guess Tracy was the last one to
          see him.

Tre fumes in anger. Noble is taken slightly off guard.

                    NOBLE
          No more questions, your honor.

Stella rises from the stand as if she could walk on clouds.
Or people. She walks by Noble who is still strongly standing
in this courtroom battle.

Noble glances at his notes and file.

                    NOBLE (CONT'D)
          The prosecution calls to the stand
          Giuseppe L'Aquila.

INT. COURTROOM - DAY

CLOSE ON a rap sheet. The pages quickly flip before our eyes.
DUIs. Resisting arrest. Assault. Battery. Lastly, a picture
and a name: GIUSEPPE L'AQUILA.

Noble flashes an optimistic smirk.

                    NOBLE
          The prosecution calls to the stand
          Giuseppe L'Aquila.

In the crowded court AUDIENCE, GIUSEPPE slowly rises.

                                        MATCH CUT TO:

INT. GT ELEMENTARY SCHOOL - GYM - DAY

Giuseppe finishes his rise and claps, teary-eyed and
cheering. He's in Giacomo Tanti Elementary's gym.

Little BALLERINAS bow onstage. One is his daughter, ANGELINA,
four or five-years old.

The moment starts to pass. Giuseppe looks around. He's the
only one standing. The few PARENTS who showed up lazily drift
into texting or light conversation.

The PIANO ACCOMPANIST lights a cigarette and leans back on
her stool.

The hoity-toity BALLET TEACHER "PSSTs" the girls off stage.

                    BALLET TEACHER
               (hushed; demeaning)
          Smiling? You think you did a good
          job? That was a disgrace! Go. Go!

Giuseppe frowns. This place is a dump.

EXT. GT ELEMENTARY SCHOOL - DAY

Parents pick up their children from the back of the gym.
Angelina rushes into Giuseppe's arms.

                    GIUSEPPE
          There you are!

                    ANGELINA
          Daddy!

Giuseppe lifts her in the air and carries her toward their car.

                    GIUSEPPE
          You were fantastic. You know that?
          FAN-TAS-TIC.

                    ANGELINA
          Really?!

                    GIUSEPPE
          Yes, you're a star! So bright and
          beautiful, you're gonna blind these
          drivers.

He playfully swoops her away, out of sight from other cars. She GIGGLES.

He puts her in his car and closes the door. Giuseppe notices the Ballet Teacher approach her car. She searches for her keys and returns to the school when she can't find them.

A few moments later... as Giuseppe's car pulls out, we reveal he slashed the Ballet Teacher's tires. The Teacher comes back, aghast and appalled.

TITLE CARD: GIUSEPPE

EXT. ICE-CREAM SHOP - DAY

Giuseppe and Angelina happily lick their ice cream.

                    GIUSEPPE
          So... you like that school?

                    ANGELINA
          Yeah!

Angelina is oblivious; her ice-cream is her entire world right now.

                    GIUSEPPE
          Sure. School's great. Learning and
          stuff.

                    ANGELINA
          Yeah.

                    GIUSEPPE
          But you like that school,
          specifically?

                    ANGELINA
          Yeah.

                    GIUSEPPE
          Got a lot of friends?

                    ANGELINA
          Yeah.

                    GIUSEPPE
          If I got you a new school, you
          could make a lot of friends there,
          too. Right?

Angelina peels her eyes from her ice-cream and looks at her
dad.

                    ANGELINA
          Yeah!

INT. COURTROOM - DAY

Giuseppe sits at the witness stand.

                    NOBLE
          Mr. L'Aquila. Sensei of Jiu-Jitsu.
          As of...

He flips through his notes.

                    NOBLE (CONT'D)
          Two months ago?

                    GIUSEPPE
          Yes.

                    NOBLE
          What'd you do before that?

                    GIUSEPPE
          Odd jobs.

EXT. CONSTRUCTION SITE - DAY

Giuseppe threateningly holds a WORKER over the ledge of a
tall building. We hear their distant YELLING and SCREAMING.

                    GIUSEPPE (V.O.)
          Construction...

INT. BAR - DAY

Giuseppe takes a baseball bat to a line of bottles, sending glass shards across the room. The BARTENDER puts his hands up in submission.

                    GIUSEPPE
          Demolition...

EXT. PALM BEACH MANSION - DAY

Carrying a long, rolled-up rug, Giuseppe and GIO (the waiter) exit the home--Godfather Part II style. They suspiciously look around, making sure no one sees them.

                    GIUSEPPE
          Remodeling...

INT. COURTROOM - DAY

Noble leans in.

                    NOBLE
          A lot of breaking stuff?

Giuseppe smiles.

                    GIUSEPPE
          Couldn't have said it better
          myself.

Giuseppe's defense attorney, AL, stands.

                    AL
          Objection, your honor. Relevance.

                    BRICKMAN
          Sustained.

                    NOBLE
               (playing to the jury)
          So you have a nice career. "Odd
          jobs." But then you go and, in
          record time, earn a black belt and
          teach karate? What happened? Change
          of heart?

Giuseppe chuckles to himself. Change of heart? Is this guy kidding?

                    NOBLE (CONT'D)
          Well, then, why'd you do it?

Giuseppe takes a long look at Al, who's face screams "Don't."

> GIUSEPPE
> Cash.

EXT. RENATA'S RISTORANTE - DAY

Giuseppe sits in his car outside RENATA'S RISTORANTE. He looks at himself in the rear-view mirror. A picture of his daughter sits on its edge.

Giuseppe fixes his hair, breathes, and points to himself.

> GIUSEPPE
> King of the jungle.

INT. RENATA'S RISTORANTE - DAY

Giuseppe walks through the restaurant and bumps past STELLA, who he hasn't met yet. He approaches a well-dressed and older guido, LOUIE who's talking to the busboys.

> GIUSEPPE
> Louie.

Louie turns around. This guy.

> LOUIE
> Sorry. Olive Garden is down the
> street.

> GIUSEPPE
> Ton' said he'd be here.

> LOUIE
> Ton' says a lot of things these
> days.

> GIUSEPPE
> Is he here or what?

> LOUIE
> You wanna meet the Don, dressed
> like that? No respect, this guy...

> TONY (O.S.)
> Giuseppe!

TONY, an old don with a raspy voice grabs Giuseppe's arm, half in affection, half for support.

> GIUSEPPE
> Hey Tony.

> TONY
> You know my zio's name was
> Giuseppe?

Tony's a bit senile.

> GIUSEPPE
> Yeah--I think you told me that
> once.

Giuseppe shoots Louie a look: "I win."

Tony leads Giuseppe away from Louie.

> TONY
> Come sit, they'll make us some
> pasta.

INT. RENATA'S RISTORANTE - MOMENTS LATER

Pasta Primavera. Giuseppe and Tony sit together. Louie and a
BODYGUARD linger nearby.

Tony eats slowly, twirling his pasta round on a spoon. He
MMMMs often, savoring each bite.

Giuseppe awkwardly watches, barely touching his food.

> GIUSEPPE
> So--

> TONY
> I love this place.

He takes another bite.

> GIUSEPPE
> Yeah. Yeah, me too. So Ton', I've
> been helping you out a while now,
> right?

> TONY
> That's right. How long's it been?
> Ten years?

> GIUSEPPE
> (lying)
> Yes. That.

                    TONY
          That's good. Loyalty's important.

                    GIUSEPPE
          Mhm. Loyalty and family, which is
          why--

                    TONY
          --Family, yeah. Hey, you know my
          zio's name was Giuseppe?

Giuseppe holds back.

                    GIUSEPPE
          It's a good name.

Tony takes another bite.

                    GIUSEPPE (CONT'D)
          Ton', I wanna earn a little more.

                    TONY
              (suddenly serious)
          More?

                    GIUSEPPE
          Lemme do some bigger work for you.

                    TONY
          How much you need?

                    GIUSEPPE
          Double.

Tony holds a stern gaze.

                    TONY
          Louie!

Louie comes over.

                    LOUIE
          Yeah?

                    TONY
          Get Giuseppe a big job.

Louie smiles. An opportunity to ruin this guy.

                    LOUIE
          My car. 3:30.

Giuseppe sighs.

EXT. DAN'S MANSION - DAY

INSERT - GIUSEPPE'S WATCH - 3:30 PM

BACK TO SCENE.

Louie and Giuseppe scope out the house from their car.
Giuseppe holds his watch in his hand and places it down in
the cup holder.

In a subtle, almost imperceptible gesture, Louie steals
Giuseppe's watch.

                    LOUIE
          Dan Jackson. He's a runner. Pilot.
          He's skimming off the top.

                    GIUSEPPE
          You want the money?

                    LOUIE
          More. Put the fear of God in him.
          He's an asset. Just a little...
          weird.

                    GIUSEPPE
          What's the catch?

Louie smiles.

                    LOUIE
          We can't find him. He's never home.

INT. COURTROOM - DAY

Noble stares at Giuseppe in disbelief.

                    NOBLE
          You got a black-belt to earn more
          cash?

                    GIUSEPPE
          Yup.

                    NOBLE
          I find it hard to believe that
          there's more money in karate than
          construction.

                    GIUSEPPE
          Yeah... the "breaking stuff" market
          wasn't going too well.

EXT. DAN'S MANSION - NIGHT

Giuseppe and GIO, a scrawny kid who's way too excited, walk
down the dimly-lit street. They're clad in all black, both
with backpacks. Giuseppe has a baseball bat.

                    GIO
          Jo, this is crazy!

                    GIUSEPPE
          Shh.

                    GIO
          Thanks for picking me for this.
          Huge honor.

                    GIUSEPPE
          You're welcome. Now shh.

                    GIO
          Seriously. You coulda picked any of
          our crew.

                    GIUSEPPE
              (sarcastic)
          Yeah, well... you're one of a kind.

They come to a hedge that surrounds Dan's mansion.

Giuseppe hands Gio binoculars.

                    GIUSEPPE (CONT'D)
          See the cameras?

                    GIO
              (through binoculars)
          Ooh, Sony PTZs. Are those 4K?

                    GIUSEPPE
          Means we gotta cut the power first.
          So... up you go.

He gestures to the telephone pole they're standing beneath.

                    GIO
          Why me?

                    GIUSEPPE
          Cause that's what I'm paying you
          for.

                    GIO
          Looks kinda old. You do it.

                    GIUSEPPE
          Gio... I'm afraid of heights. All
          right?

                    GIO
          Really?!

                    GIUSEPPE
          Yes, really. Now get up there.

                    GIO
          I want extra for this.

                    GIUSEPPE
          How much.

                    GIO
              (dead serious)
          Thirty. Dollars.

Is this kid for real?

                    GIUSEPPE
          That's a tough one. I'll pay. Now
          get up there!

Gio scurries up the pole.

                    GIO
          And here... we... go.

He cuts a cable. The mansion's lights stay on.

                    GIUSEPPE
          It didn't work!

                    GIO
          Shoot... I think that was the
          nursing home cross the street.

                    GIUSEPPE
          Focus, kid!

Gio cuts another cable and the mansion's lights go out.

                    GIO
          Tada!

Giuseppe lifts his bat and pats it as he walks toward the
house. Batter up.

INT. DAN'S MANSION - LIVING ROOM - THE NEXT DAY

                    STELLA
          AHH!!!

Broken coffee table, shattered glass, smashed TV.

Stella, in her morning robe, dials a number.

EXT. DAN'S MANSION - DAY

A white van sits on the road in front of Dan's mansion.

INT. TECH VAN - DAY

Gio and Giuseppe huddle around a pair of headphones,
listening in on a call.

                    DANIEL (V.O.)
          Did they take anything?

                    STELLA (V.O.)
          No... but--

                    DANIEL (V.O.)
          Are you hurt?

                    STELLA (V.O.)
          No. But Dan--

                    DANIEL (V.O.)
          Then what are you screaming about?

                    STELLA (V.O.)
          I WAS HOME ALONE! Someone broke in
          and I was ALONE!

                    DANIEL (V.O.)
          What do you want from me?

Gio leans back laughing.

                    GIO
          This boy's in trouble!

                    GIUSEPPE
          Shh!

                    STELLA (V.O.)
          I don't feel safe. You need to come
          home, that's what you need to do.

Giuseppe looks at Gio, optimistic.

                    DANIEL (V.O.)
          I will. In a few weeks.

                    STELLA (V.O)
          Weeks?!

                    GIUSEPPE
          Weeks?!

Giuseppe covers his mouth, realizing he just said that into
the phone.

                    DANIEL (V.O.)
          I've got a few more runs to make
          this month. Till then I'll be in
          and out.

                    STELLA (V.O.)
          Dan...

                    DANIEL (V.O.)
          Just hire someone to stay at the
          house with you.

Lightbulb: Giuseppe half-smirks.

EXT. DAN'S MANSION - DAY

KNOCK, KNOCK, KNOCK. Giuseppe stands at the door wearing an
interview suit, carrying a briefcase.

He curiously eyes the BIG YELLOW BUS sitting in the driveway.

Stella and Diane answers the door in professional clothes.
But she's struck by Giuseppe. He's so tall. And handsome.

                    STELLA
               (clearing her throat)
          Come in.

INT. DAN'S MANSION - DINNING ROOM

Stella and her friend DIANE sit across from Giuseppe,
interview style, with notepads and questions. They're both a
little nervous and jittery.

                    GIUSEPPE
          That's a big bus you've got out
          there.

                    DIANE
               (smitten)
          Yeah.

Stella rolls her eyes at Diane.

                    STELLA
               (reading)
          Joe... L'Aquila?

                    DIANE
          Is that French?

Giuseppe sighs.

                    GIUSEPPE
          No, ma'am.

                    STELLA
               (to Diane)
          It's Italian, bimbo.
               (to Giuseppe)
          So you're a professional bodyguard.

                    GIUSEPPE
          Yeah. Sure.

                    DIANE
          What formal training do you have?

                    GIUSEPPE
          Like fighting?

                    STELLA
          Yes, kickboxing, army...

                    GIUSEPPE
               (lying)
          Oh yeah, I do, uh Karate, mostly.

                    DIANE
          Karate?!

She eyes Stella, knowingly.

                    STELLA
          I've always wanted to learn!

Diane eyes her again, "No you haven't!"

                    GIUSEPPE
          Oh it's not hard. You could do it,
          easy.

                    DIANE
          Could you teach us? Uh--Her?

                    GIUSEPPE
          Yes. Yeah.

Diane gives Stella an affirmative look. Stella looks back at
her notes.

                    STELLA
          So, would you consider yourself a
          protective person?

                    GIUSEPPE
          Yeah. I've got a little girl.
          Angie.

Giuseppe can't help but smile.

                    GIUSEPPE (CONT'D)
          She can't protect herself, ya know?
          When people don't treat her right,
          it don't make me happy. So I do
          what I gotta do.

                    DIANE
                (suspicious)
          What do you do?

                    GIUSEPPE
          Uh, well. To be honest, the reason
          I took this job... want to take
          this job is to get her a better
          school.

Stella and Diane smile. This guy is adorable!

INT. KARATE DOJO - DAY

SENSEI KEVIN, Mr. Nerd himself, enters the Dojo with
Giuseppe.

                    SENSEI KEVIN
          It's great to train someone who's
          so... large!

                    GIUSEPPE
          What?

                    SENSEI KEVIN
          Well most of the guys I teach
          are... well...

He gestures to himself.

                    GIUSEPPE
          Oh.

                    SENSEI KEVIN
          Thanks for being a trendsetter.
          Karate's really for everyone.

                    GIUSEPPE
          Uh-huh.

                    SENSEI KEVIN
          It all starts with your horse
          stance. Like this.

Sensei Kevin spreads his legs wide. Giuseppe takes out a
paper and pen and writes something down.

                    SENSEI KEVIN (CONT'D)
          Ah, studious!

                    GIUSEPPE
              (to himself; writing)
          Horse Dance.

                    SENSEI KEVIN
          No, no. Horse Stance.

                    GIUSEPPE
          Sure, sure. What else?

Giuseppe takes a horse stance.

                    SENSEI KEVIN
          It's all about balance. When
          striking your foe or taking a blow,
          you need to keep balance.

                    GIUSEPPE
          What if you use a baseball bat?

Awkward beat. Then Sensei Kevin erupts into laughter, tapping
Giuseppe.

Giuseppe play-laughs along.

INT. DAN'S MANSION - LIVING ROOM

Giuseppe spreads his legs into a horse stance. Stella
observes carefully.

                    GIUSEPPE
          This is your horse dance.

                    STELLA
          Horse dance?

                    GIUSEPPE
          Yeah, it's the way ponies look when
          they dance with each other.

                    STELLA
          Oh.

Stella forms a horse stance.

                    GIUSEPPE
          Good. It's all about balance,
          remember. Gotta keep your peace and
          stuff.

                    STELLA
          Peace. Wonder what that's like.

                    GIUSEPPE
          Rough day?

                    STELLA
          Rough month.

They eye each other. A beat of tension and romance.

INT. INTERROGATION ROOM - DAY

Giuseppe sits alone in the quiet room.

                    GIUSEPPE
          You gonna ask any questions?

                    MARCUS
          Nope.

Marcus leans back with a cup of coffee and the morning paper.

Giuseppe's uncomfortable with all this. Something's wrong.

                    GIUSEPPE
          So you gonna let me go?

                    MARCUS
          Nope.

                    GIUSEPPE
          Look, I don't know why I'm here.
          I'm just a security guy.

                    MARCUS
               (sarcastic)
          That's interesting.

                    GIUSEPPE
          Ask Stel... ask Mrs. Jackson.
          She'll tell you.

Marcus looks up, interested.

                    MARCUS
          Were you and Mrs. Jackson--

INT. COURTROOM - DAY

                    NOBLE
          --Close?

                    GIUSEPPE
          Yeah, she's alright.

Giuseppe looks to Stella in the gallery.

                    NOBLE
          Were there any feelings of romance
          between you two?

                    GIUSEPPE
          Where there's heat, there's fire.
          Know what I'm saying?

GASPING and MURMURING in the court.

                    NOBLE
          As an employer, did Mrs. Jackson
          pay on time?

                    GIUSEPPE
          Yeah.

INT. DAN'S MANSION - LIVING ROOM - DAY

                    GIUSEPPE (V.O.)
          Paid pretty well, too.

Stella closes a drawer.

                         STELLA
               I can't find my check book. You
               okay with cash?

Giuseppe's eyes twinkle; he forgot about being paid.

Stella pulls twenty benjamins from her wallet and hands the
cash to Giuseppe who glances it over. Not bad.

                         STELLA (CONT'D)
               Won't need you tomorrow. I'll be
               out with Diane.

INT. DAN'S MANSION - ENTRANCE - THE NEXT DAY

The front door unlocks and creaks open. Giuseppe pops his
head in, scouting the area.

                         GIUSEPPE
               Hello?

After a silent beat, Giuseppe's head withdraws.

                         GIUSEPPE (O.S.) (CONT'D)
               Go.

In walks Angelina, wearing a bathing suit and floaties. She
tip toes further in, followed by Giuseppe.

EXT. POOL - DAY

SPLASH! Angelina floats to the surface and splashes around.

                         ANGELINA
               Daddy, come play with me!

                         GIUSEPPE
               Two minutes, angel.

Giuseppe's seated at an outdoor table, beneath a white
umbrella. On the table are dozens of pamphlets, Stella's
cash, scratch paper, and a pencil. Giuseppe picks up a
pamphlet.

INSERT - PAMPHLET 1

Veria Christian School. A nice-looking place. Smiling faces.
Tuition = $10,620

BACK TO SCENE.

Giuseppe nods. Seems reasonable. His phone RINGS. He answers.

                    GIUSEPPE (CONT'D)
          Yeah?

                    LOUIE (V.O.)
          Checking in, how's it going?

                    GIUSEPPE
               (lying)
          Not too great.

Giuseppe ironically lifts his stack of cash and puts it away.
He picks up another pamphlet.

                    GIUSEPPE (CONT'D)
          Doesn't look like this job's gonna
          work out.

INSERT - PAMPHLET 2

Monarch's Academy. Nicer. Much nicer. Concert hall with lots
of young ballerinas. Tuition = $19,250

BACK TO SCENE.

Giuseppe recoils. Oof.

                    LOUIE (V.O.)
          Ton' won't be too happy bout that.
          Means no pay for you. I'll let him
          know.

                    GIUSEPPE
          Wait.

Giuseppe looks to Angelina, still splashing around the pool.

                    GIUSEPPE (CONT'D)
          I'll keep at it.

INT. COURTROOM - DAY

                    NOBLE
          Where were you on June 8th?

Giuseppe looks to his attorney. Big moment.

INT. DAN'S MANSION - ENTRANCE

Giuseppe enters the house.

                    GIUSEPPE
               (calling out)
          Just me, Mrs. Jackson.

He leaves the door slightly open when he hears muffled
arguing. It's Stella's voice and another's... a man's
voice...

Game time.

Giuseppe moves stealthily across the house, toward the source
of the arguing. Someone's coming!

Giuseppe ducks out of sight, now in the kitchen. Stella
enters, frantic. Giuseppe watches carefully as she takes a
pair of scissors and rushes out the back door.

Giuseppe's eyes go wide. He follows her.

EXT. AIRFIELD - DAY

Stella wrenches open a panel on the side of the plane and
readies her scissors to cut.

                    GIUSEPPE
          What are you doing?!

Stella's shocked.

                    STELLA
          I... uh...

Giuseppe grabs her and carries her back to the house.

                    STELLA (CONT'D)
          Let go of me! I need to do this!

INT. DAN'S MANSION - LIVING ROOM

Stella's tied up. She struggles to break free.

                    GIUSEPPE
          Don't move.

INT. COURTROOM - DAY

                    GIUSEPPE
          I was at the house. Me and Stella
          were... together. Dan walks in on
          us, in a very compromising
          position.

INT. DAN'S MANSION - DAY

Dan walks in on Giuseppe putting duct tape over Stella's
mouth.

                    GIUSEPPE
          Keep quiet!

Giuseppe realizes Dan's here.

                    GIUSEPPE (CONT'D)
          Don Longo sends his regards.

                    DANIEL
          Tre, run.

Tre leaves as Dan throws a punch at Giuseppe. The massive man
goes unmoved.

After realizing that his punches won't do any good, he tries
to flee. Giuseppe takes vases and lamps and throws them at
Dan, knocking him to the floor. Their fight leads them
outside.

INT. COURTROOM - DAY

                    GIUSEPPE
          So we get into a little fight is
          all.

                    NOBLE
          And who won the fight?

Giuseppe's offended.

                    GIUSEPPE
          Who do you think?

EXT. DAN'S MANSION - YARD/AIRFIELD - DAY

Giuseppe pursues Dan, who flees full speed out of the house.

                    GIUSEPPE (V.O.)
          The guy runs away. Some husband. So
          I let 'em.

He doesn't. Giuseppe sprints after Dan.

Tre reenters and sees the chaos.

Dan turns to fight Giuseppe, running out of options. He spots
Tre.

                    DANIEL
          Kid, get outta here!!!

A few more punches, dodges, and swipes. Dan is knocked to the
ground. As Giuseppe's about to make another devastating
hit...

GASOLINE sprays in Giuseppe's face! Tre stayed and saved Dan.
Giuseppe falls down in a coughing fit.

                    DANIEL (CONT'D)
          Thanks. Now really, go!

Tre drops the gas pump and runs off as Dan threateningly
lights a match! He looks at the match, then to Giuseppe
covered in gasoline.

                    DANIEL (CONT'D)
               (comedic beat)
          That's a bit much.

Dan waves out the match and runs for his plane.

CLOSE ON GIUSEPPE. Fuming. He aggressively leaves frame, in
the direction of Dan.

                    GIUSEPPE (V.O.)
          Never saw him again.

INT. COURTROOM - DAY

Giuseppe leaves the witness stand and takes his seat. Noble
also returns to his seat. We hold on him. He's exhausted. He
thumbs through his notes, frustrated.

                    BRICKMAN
          Does the prosecution rest?

Something catches Noble's eye. A yellow mail package.

                    BRICKMAN (CONT'D)
          Mr. Noble. Does the prosecution
          rest?

Noble opens the package and peers inside. His face flushes
with revelation. He stands.

                    NOBLE
          One last thing, your honor!

                                        CUT TO BLACK.

INT. COURTROOM - DAY

The courtroom is a buzz as the JURY reenters. TRE looks to
MS. JOY and HAZEL. STELLA stands up in a panic. GIUSEPPE is
stoic and brooding.

BRICKMAN slams his gavel.

> BRICKMAN
> Order! We will have Order! Mr.
> Freeman, Mrs. Jackson, Mr.
> L'Aquila, please rise. Members of
> the jury, have you arrived at a
> verdict.

> FOREPERSON
> Yes, your honor. In light of the
> late evidence presented by Mr.
> Noble and Detective Bjornson, we
> the jury, on the charge of murder
> in the first degree on June 8th,
> find the defendant Tracy Freeman
> not guilty. As to Stella Jackson,
> the jury finds you not guilty. As
> to Giuseppe L'Aquila, the jury
> finds you guilty.

> GIUSEPPE
> Hey, I didn't do nothing! I...
> Louie you...

> BRICKMAN
> Bailiff, please take Mr. L'Aquila
> into custody.

The BAILIFF attempts to apprehend Giuseppe, but he crashes
like a wave on a coastal cliff. Another officer of the court
rushes to help his colleague.

The court erupts in chaos. Giuseppe YELLS in defiance of the
court. Stella is out of the courtroom before the gallery is
even out of their seats. Detective Bjornson grabs Tre from
his seat.

> MARCUS
> Come with me right now!

Bjornson rushes Tre out of the courtroom.

THE WRECK OF ECHO 10-4

INT. PARKING GARAGE - DAY

An animated Tre protests Detective Bjornson. Bjornson,
unphased by Tre's gestures, hurries to the back of the
parking garage and stops as a black Mercedes pulls around the
corner and flashes its lights at the men.

                    TRE
          What kind of James Bond...

The car window drops down and a familiar face with aviator
sunglasses pops out the window.

                    DANIEL
          Come on kid, I got a plane to
          catch!

Tre pauses in disbelief.

                    DANIEL (CONT'D)
          Yea, I'm not dead. It's not that
          surprising. Let's go.

                    TRE
          This dude...

Tre runs and enters the vehicle.

EXT. PARKING GARAGE - MOMENTS LATER

From above we see the black Mercedes pull out onto the
street. After a few beats we see a nice sports car pull out
onto the street and turn in the same direction as the black
Mercedes.

INT. DAN'S CAR - DAY

Dan drives the car down the freeway into a heavily wooded
area. Detective Bjornson monitors police radios in the back
seat of the car. Tre stares at Dan in disbelief in the
passenger seat.

                    DANIEL
          What, no hello?

                    TRE
              (shocked)
          Hel... Hello?

Tre shoves Dan in anger. The car swerves on the highway.
Marcus works from the back as if nothing is happening.

                    TRE (CONT'D)
          I'ma say hello to your corpse! I
          almost got put away for good, and
          you want a stupid 'Hello'?

                    DANIEL
          We'll all be corpses if you don't
          stop.

Tre continues to shove Dan and now starts punching him.
Marcus sends an email on his laptop.

                    MARCUS
          This is going well.

                    DANIEL
          Alright, stop already!

Tre relents his bombardment and sits back in his chair.

                    TRE
          What happened man? It's been...
          well, you know.

                    DANIEL
          But you're still here aren't ya
          kid.

                    TRE
          No thanks to you.

                    MARCUS
          True--I'll take credit for that.
          You're welcome.

                    TRE
          You? The guy who arrested and
          almost locked me up for good? Why
          are you even here?

                    DANIEL
          Marcus is an old Air Force buddy of
          mine.

                    TRE
              (in disbelief)
          Air For... Buddy?! You know what?
          Let me out. Pullover.

Tre takes his seat belt off and attempts to get out of the
car.

                    DANIEL
          Calm down.

THE WRECK OF ECHO 10-4

                         MARCUS
                    (under his breath)
               Click-it or ticket.

                         TRE
               I'm not going to calm down until
               you tell me what's going on.

The three men sit quietly in the car for a second. Marcus
closes his laptop, Tre stares at Dan, Dan stares out onto the
road. Dan removes his aviator glasses.

                         DANIEL
               Here's what happened.

TITLE CARD: DAN

EXT. AIRFIELD - DAY

Dan Jackson narrates from inside the scene with Tre. We will
call them PRESENT DAN and TRE.

PAST DAN JACKSON stands on stage in his military uniform.
Lights flash as REPORTERS snap their cameras at the war hero.
A GENERAL walks on stage to present Dan with a medal. A
happy, but stoic PAST MARCUS BJORNSON stands just behind his
friend. Present Dan and Tre stand in the crowd.

                         DANIEL
               Over 200 combat missions flown in
               Iraq, second only to Lt. Col.
               Uribe.

Past Dan receives his medal and turns to Past Bjornson.
Stella runs up and gives Past Dan a kiss.

Present Dan turns to Tre.

                         DANIEL (CONT'D)
               Imagine your heart beating out of
               your chest as you fly eighteen-
               hundred miles per hour in a fighter
               jet. But now you're sitting at a
               desk eight-hours a day.

INT. RENATA'S RISTORANTE - DAY

Past Dan in his Aviator jacket and glasses walks up to TONY
LONGO, seated at his usual table, surrounded by bodyguards
and Louie.

Present Dan and Tre sit in the corner of the back of the room.

> **TRE**
> The mob? Yo, and I thought I was a criminal.

> **DANIEL**
> I didn't join. I just needed a hobby to keep me busy.

> **TRE**
> (sarcastic)
> Oh yeah, having a hobby is important.

Tre shakes his head in disapproval. Past Dan shakes hands with Tony. Louie drops a big bag of cash.

> **DANIEL**
> Especially one that pays.

EXT. COASTAL HIGHWAY - CONVERTIBLE CAR - DAY

Past Dan and Stella cruise down a coastal highway in a fancy convertible sports car. Stella raises her hands in the air. Past Dan smiles as he speeds down the road.

Present Dan and Tre sit in the back seat of the convertible.

> **TRE**
> And almost sending a city boy to jail comes in...?

> **DANIEL**
> I had it all, kid. Beautiful wife, nice car, money.

INT. DAN'S MANSION - LIVING ROOM - DAY

A bored and melancholy Past Dan sits on an expensive sofa. We move out from the isolated man, revealing the luxury of the room plus an excited Stella pacing, TALKING on the phone.

Present Dan and Tre stand on the other side of the room.

> **DANIEL**
> And it ruined me, or so I thought anyway. I just felt... trapped you know?

                    TRE
          If that's what being trapped looks
          like, feel free to trap me.

                    DANIEL
          I needed the rush and thrill of
          being on the edge.

EXT. UNKNOWN AIRFIELD - NIGHT

Past Dan leans over into his plane. He opens a large duffel
bag filled with cash. He shuffles the money around and then
looks over his shoulder at an empty hangar in the distance.
Past Dan pulls some of the money out of the bag and stashes
it in the siding of the plane.

Past Dan walks into the empty hangar carrying the duffel bag.
He opens a container filled with similar duffel bags to the
one he's carrying.

Present Dan and Tre watch from a distance hiding behind some
boxes in the hangar. Past Dan looks around again, tosses the
bag into the container, and runs back to the plane.

                    TRE
          So you decide to steal from the one
          group of people you should probably
          never steal from?

                    DANIEL
          I hopped back into my plane and
          flew until the sun came up.

INT. AIRPLANE - SUNRISE

A smiling Past Dan stares into the sunset. He looks back into
the cabin of the plane where he tucked away the money. He
looks forward and CHEERS excitingly.

                    DANIEL (V.O.)
          The adrenaline. The thrill. I was
          back.

EXT. CABIN - DAY

Back in the present, Dan's car pulls up to an old rustic
cabin in the middle of the woods. The structure is older, but
well maintained. The property is contained by a medium sized
fence. Heavy equipment riddles the outskirts of the
territory.

The three men step out of the vehicle. Tre leans on the side of the car.

> TRE
> And then...

> DANIEL
> Then I got a call from Stella.

EXT. MILITARY BAR - NIGHT

Motorcycles and rough looking men linger outside a small bar. The men wear American flag bandanas and have military patches on their vests and jackets. They laugh and joke around as they drink and smoke cigarettes.

Dan stands off from the bar and paces the parking lot as he talks on the phone with Stella. Present Dan and Tre lean on a car in the parking lot.

> DANIEL (V.O)
> Someone smashed up the house. I
> should have gone home but, I
> figured this might have to do
> something with the money. So, I
> lied. Said I was gonna be out of
> town for a couple of weeks.

> DANIEL (CONT'D)
> I've got a few more runs to make
> this month. Till then I'll be in
> and out.

Beat.

> DANIEL (CONT'D)
> Just hire someone to stay at the
> house with you.

EXT. STREET - DAY

Dan covertly cruises down the street to his house. He wears a baseball cap and Aviator glasses to conceal his face. He looks to his left and notices a group of ELDERLY PEOPLE hanging outside of their building.

The old folks lay out on lawn chairs. One older man raises his phone to the sky attempting to figure out how to use it. An older woman yells at a caretaker.

> OLD LADY
> When will the power be back!

> CARE TAKER
> Do I look like an electrician?

Dan watches the scene from the road and then looks at the cut power lines near his house.

> DANIEL (V.O.)
> It was only a matter of time till
> they would track me down.

INT. CABIN - KITCHEN - DAY

The three men stand in the cabin kitchen. The cabin is large and rustic but does not lack the modern amenities of leisure. Dan leans over on the counter directing his conversation at Tre. Tre lowers his glass of water and looks at Dan.

Dan leans on the counter and turns his attention towards Bjornson.

> DANIEL
> So I turned to the best wing-man in
> the United States Air Force.

> MARCUS
> When a friend is ready to walk the
> straight and narrow, it's only
> proper to help him out.

INT. POLICE OFFICE - NIGHT

Detective Marcus Bjornson earnestly studies his laptop on his desk. The detective's office is clean, neat, and perfectly balanced in decor.

Bjornson pulls out a list of files labeled "Tony Longo" and drops them on his desk.

> MARCUS (V.O.)
> I was already building a case
> against the Longo family. And I had
> the perfect rat.

Bjornson opens the file revealing a photo of Louie De Luca.

EXT. ALLEYWAY - DAY

Past Bjornson leans up against a wall in an alleyway. Present Tre and Bjornson sit on a bench across the street watching the alleyway. Louie walks up and greets the Detective. Louie dials a number into the phone.

                    LOUIE
               (into phone)
          Checking in, how's it going?

                    MARCUS
          After Dan told me about the
          blackout, I knew that Longo's man
          was on him, so I reached out to my
          contact. Had him update on his
          progress.

                    DANIEL
          The Mob was after me, my wife was
          spending all my money--driving me
          crazy. What better way to escape my
          problems than to fake my own death
          and start over new?

Detective Bjornson looks down in disappointment. Tre steps
back and shakes his head.

                    TRE
          What happened to putting in the
          work and not being a victim? Even I
          know, you can't run away from your
          problems.

                    DANIEL
          But you can parachute.

INT. COCKPIT - DAY

                    DANIEL
          Mayday, mayday, this is Echo 10-4!
          I've lost control of my plane!

Dan flicks his cigarette out of the side of the plane and
then jumps out of the plane himself.

EXT. FOREST - DAY

The plane slowly descends to the ocean. As Dan rushes towards
the earth he pulls his parachute and abruptly slows into a
glide. The plane smashes into the sea.

Dan tosses a sinister smile as the crash explosion is seen
through his aviator glasses.

INT. CABIN - KITCHEN - DAY

                    MARCUS
It should've looked like a freak-
accident, or suicide. There wasn't
supposed to be a trial.

                    DANIEL
But I did lose control of the
plane. Engine overheated. Oil
compressor failed. Someone tried to
murder me.

                    MARCUS
Giuseppe had the clear motive.

INT. POLICE OFFICE - NIGHT

Louie places GIUSEPPE'S WATCH on Marcus' desk. Marcus lifts
it and smiles.

                    MARCUS
Louie gave me a valuable piece of
evidence to plant against Giuseppe,
and he promised to testify against
him.

INT. CABIN - KITCHEN - DAY

                    TRE
So you framed the guy?

                    DANIEL
He tried to kill me on the
airfield. You saw it!

                    MARCUS
                (to Tre)
But since you wouldn't testify to
having stayed, the jury couldn't
know that.

Tre takes a guilty beat.

                    TRE
What about the will?

                    DANIEL
How do you know about the will?

                    MARCUS
It came up in court.

                    TRE
          You put me in your will, but you
          barely know me.

Dan turns away from the group and rubs his head in
preparation for another hard revelation.

                    DANIEL
          That day in the airport. Stella
          called me selfish and...

                    TRE
              (hurt)
          You wanted to prove her wrong?

                    MARCUS
          Here we go.

                    DANIEL
          Yeah. Spite her, you know?

Tre looks away in disbelief.

                    DANIEL (CONT'D)
          Lighten up, Tre. I did a lot for
          you, didn't I?

                    TRE
          Yo, Stella was right. You're just
          some selfish rich dude.

Heaviness and silence once again fill the room. Suddenly,
something clicks in Tre's mind.

                    TRE (CONT'D)
          You said the engine overheated?
          That happened in my flight test,
          too. And there was only one person
          who was there both days.

BAM! The wall SHATTERS into a million pieces. The men are
thrown to the ground by the force of a BUS bursting through
the wall. Smoke and debris fill the room.

An enraged but well put together STELLA gracefully walks out
of the bus with her stolen handgun!

                    STELLA
          Knock, knock.

Tre struggles to get up and coughs as debris falls off of his
back. Detective Bjornson is unconscious on the floor. From
the floor, Dan spots Marcus's radio.

Dan crawls towards the radio but when a SHOT is fired he
slowly rolls over on to his back and looks up at Stella.

                    DANIEL
          Ah Stel! You look beautiful as
          always.

                    STELLA
          I know. Now get up!

Stella grabs Dan and pulls him to his feet. She shoves him
backwards while keeping her gun aimed at him.

                    DANIEL
          Didn't see that on the bank
          statement.

                    STELLA
          I stole it.

Tre attempts to sneak out the side of the room. Stella moves
the gun in his direction.

                    STELLA (CONT'D)
          And where is my partner in crime
          going?

                    DANIEL
          Partner?

                    TRE
          Oh, hey Mrs. Jackson! It's good to
          see you again. This just looks like
          a family issue, so I'll step out.

                    STELLA
          As much as you've been at our
          house? Oh please sweetie, you're
          practically family. Stay.

                    TRE
          Nah, I insist--

Stella sends another round into the roof.

                    TRE (CONT'D)
          Yes, ma'am.

Tre slumps over to stand next to Dan. Marcus moans on the
ground. Stella bends down and picks up the detective's radio
and gun.

Dan slips a small closed envelope into Tre's hand. Tre hides
it in his sleeve.

                    STELLA
          I'd love to let sweet Tre go, but
          there's one tiny quarter million
          dollar problem.

                    TRE
          I don't want a dime of this fool's
          money. Y'all have a nice life.

Tre begins to walk out of the room again. Stella FIRES
another shot. Tre hops back to Dan's side.

Bjornson slowly opens his eye and continues to play dead as
he assesses the situation.

                    TRE (CONT'D)
          Dang, this lady's really upset.

                    DANIEL
          Seriously Stel, that's all you care
          about?

                    STELLA
          I'm not that shallow.

                    TRE
          Got me fooled.

                    STELLA
          I want someone to eat dinner with.
          Someone to binge an overhyped TV
          show with. Someone to be there when
          I get home from shopping!

                    DANIEL
          I'm right here, babe.

                    STELLA
          Only because I'm swinging a gun in
          your face. Otherwise, you'd be off
          with him somewhere.

Stella gestures with her gun to Tre.

                    TRE
          He only spent time with me to spite
          you. He's a selfish rich jerk just
          like you said.

                    DANIEL
               (under breath)
          Thanks, Tre.

                    STELLA
          When Dan first told me about you...
          He wasn't even that excited on our
          wedding day. Every day it was, "Tre
          this" and "Tre that" and "He's
          gonna be the best pilot."

She slowly approaches Tre.

                    STELLA (CONT'D)
          All his attention was on some city
          kid with no future. I want my
          money. And I want my husband back!

She points and cocks the gun at Tre.

                    DANIEL
          Stella don't!

Tre is frozen in place as he stares at the gun pointed at him
across the room. Stella closes her eyes and pulls the
trigger, just as Marcus tackles her to the ground.

The guns trajectory is thrown off by the scuffle. Tre braces
for his fate, but Dan just makes it in time to shove Tre out
of the path of the bullet! The round plants itself into Dan,
who collapses to the floor.

                    TRE
          Dan! Dan!!!

                    DANIEL
               (wounded)
          Now I remember why I joined the
          Chairforce.

                    TRE
          What's wrong with you man!

                    DANIEL
          A lot of things. I'm sorry, Tre.
          You're a real pilot. You logged all
          those flight hours, you landed that
          broken plane.

Dan gestures to the envelope he gave Tre.

                    DANIEL (CONT'D)
          This your chance to take control of
          your life, and shape your future.
          How far you go... it's up to you.

Tre pulls the envelope out of his sleeve.

                    DANIEL (CONT'D)
                 (nearly unconscious)
            Fly on, Tre.

A dazed Marcus stands to his feet. While on the ground Stella
notices the guns have slid underneath the debris of the
house. She stands to her feet to face Marcus.

Marcus attempts to grab and restrain her. Stella grabs
Marcus's lead arm, plants her feet shoulder width apart, and
rotates her weight and Bjornsons' around the outside of her
body, hip tossing the detective straight to the ground.
Stella slowly exhales and holds her stance.

                    STELLA
            Horse Dance!

Stella looks across the room and notices Tre holding an
envelope from Dan. Tre makes eye contact with Stella. A beat.

Tre takes off out the house.

EXT. CABIN - DAY

Tre busts out the back door of the house and looks around for
a path of egress. He runs towards a medium sized fence across
the yard. Stella knocks down the door Tre exited, and sprints
after Tre.

                    STELLA
            Give me the envelope, Tre!

                    TRE
            Gotta take it from me, tonto!

Tre reaches the tall fence and jumps onto it. He struggles to
get over it, but makes it over just as Stella catches up to
him. Tre spots and dashes toward a dirt bike at the end of
the fence line.

                    TRE (CONT'D)
            Don't worry! Your skin will look
            great in that prison orange!

Tre's laughter is cut short when he notices Stella flying
over the top of the fence with ease.

Tre panics and hops on the bike. As Stella runs towards the
bike she notices a baseball bat laying along the fence and
grabs it.

Tre kicks the kick-starter several times.

                        TRE (CONT'D)
          Come on...

Stella closes the distance on Tre and reels the bat
backwards. The engine of the bike roars into rhythm as Tre
ducks underneath the bat swing and smashes the throttle
forward. The bike takes off and Tre is carried out of the
yard and onto the street.

EXT. FOREST STREET - DAY

Tre continues to look back and see if he is pursued. He slows
down to catch his breath and get his bearings. As he glances
at the envelope in his pocket, Stella, driving Dan's car,
bursts onto the street. Tre ramps up the throttle and
continues forward.

Stella flies down the road in her car. She catches up to Tre
and drives alongside of him. Tre looks at Stella, and then
looks at the road, and then back at Stella.

                        TRE
          Don't do it.

Stella swerves the car at Tre, who swerves to keep from being
bumped by the car. Stella swerves the car again at Tre. She
manages to bump the front of the dirt bike forcing Tre to
fight to keep balance on the Bike.

Stella makes eye contact with the envelope in Tre's pocket.
She aggressively swerves and makes contact with Tre. Tre
flies off the road and disappears.

Stella slams on her breaks and peers over the edge of the
road to see if she can see the wreckage. Tre's bike flies
into the air as he takes his vehicle off a makeshift ramp and
into an abandoned off-road dirt park.

Stella grits her teeth and drives her car into the park.

EXT. OFFROAD PARK - DAY

Tre SCREAMS as he fights to maintain control of his bike. He
flies off another short dirt ramp and into a race track.
Stella's car bursts onto a track out of a cloud of dirt.

Tre races around the track looking for a way to evade
Stella's car. Stella continues in her pursuit but she's
having a difficult time trying the navigate the course in her
luxury sports car.

Tre looks ahead and spots a wide elevated turn on the course.
He looks behind and notices Stella fighting to keep her eyes
on him. Tre slows down his bike and maneuvers in front of
Stella.

The dirt kicks up and blocks Stella's view. She turns on the
window wipers in hopes of aiding her vision. Tre leads Stella
up to the edge of the turn and swerves back down into the
course.

As Stella's vision clears she notices she's heading off the
edge of a turn, but its to late.

The car flies off of the course and rolls down to the ground.
Tre drives up to the edge of the turn and stares down at the
car. Stella lies unconscious in the car.

                                              FADE OUT.

EXT. OFFROAD PARK - DUSK

Two POLICEMEN escort Stella into a police car.

                    STELLA
          You've got the wrong girl. I would
          never hurt anyone!

Detective Bjornson, who is now rocking a sling, hangs up his
cell phone. He approaches Tre, who's handcuffed and sitting
on the side of the road.

                    TRE
          Is Dan?

Marcus stands up Tre and uncuffs him.

                    TRE (CONT'D)
          What are you doing?

                    MARCUS
          Congratulations. You're a "free-
          man."

                    TRE
          Seriously, how's Dan?

                    MARCUS
          Dan? He died in a plane crash.
          Remember?

Detective Bjornson begins to walk away from Tre. Tre just
stares the Detective. Marcus stops and turns around to face
Tre.

                    MARCUS (CONT'D)
          You dropped something out there--on
          the track.

Detective Bjornson tosses the envelope to Tre. Tre catches
the envelope and grips it gently in his hands.

                    MARCUS (CONT'D)
          Stay out of trouble.

Marcus walks back to the ensemble of OFFICERS, PARAMEDICS,
and FIREFIGHTERS. Tre quickly opens the envelope and pulls
out the will.

INSERT: DAN'S WILL

TRACY FREEMAN. PLANE. $250,000.00

BACK TO SCENE.

Tre pulls out the GPS and keys. He holds the GPS to his face
in confusion.

EXT. ABANDONED HANGAR - DAY

Tre lowers the GPS from his face and stares at the abandoned
hangar in front of him.

Tre slides the hangar door open. The door CREAKS and SCREAMS
as months of rust and dirt are pushed through the pulley.

                    TRE
               (underbreath)
          Whoa!

We reveal a brand new plane. Tre runs up and opens the door
to the plane. Inside there are stuffed bags of cash.

Tre almost passes out in disbelief. He grabs a note that is
sitting in the cockpit.

INSERT: NOTE

MAKE IT COUNT, KID.

BACK TO SCENE.

As Tre finishes reading the note, an AIRPLANE flies over the
hangar. Tre runs out of the hangar and stares at the sky. The
camera circles around Tre as he searches the sky for his
mentor.

                                        FADE TO BLACK.

INT. PRISON CELL - DAY

Giuseppe sits on his jail cell bunk in an orange jump suit. A
intimidating MONSTER OF A MAN sits next to him on the bunk.
Giuseppe studies the physique of the man.

                    GIUSEPPE
          So... you like it here?

The inmate maintains eye contact of his knuckles. Admiring
the wear and tear of his bones.

                    INMATE 3
          Yeah.

                    GIUSEPPE
          Got a lot of friends?

                    INMATE 3
          Yeah.

                    GIUSEPPE
          But, if I got you out of here you
          probably could make a lot of new
          friends right?

The hulking inmate inquisitively looks over at Giuseppe.

                    INMATE 3
          Yeah!

Suddenly, Detective Bjornson approaches the cell, whistling.

                    GIUSEPPE
          You!

Bjornson ignores him and continues whistling as he
"accidentally" drops a ring of keys onto the cell floor. Then
Bjornson walks away.

Giuseppe and Inmate 3 eye each other.

EXT. PRISON - DAY

SIRENS and DOGS sound off as the camera cranes away from the
facility.

INT. PRISON - PHONE BOOTH - DAY

A no make-up and unkempt hair Stella rocks an orange jump-
suit and plain white shoes. She leans on the wall as she
talks into a phone.

                    STELLA
          Dios mio, Diane! I'm telling you,
          you would absolutely love it here.
          I started making nail polish from
          printer ink I stole from the
          warden's office and pawning them to
          the ladies in cell block D, and
          now, they love me!... I know,
          chiquita! It's like I have my own
          little prison bi-

BURKE bangs the phone booth.

                    BURKE (O.S.)
          Hey, time's up!

Stella sighs.

                    STELLA
          Tell me about it, Dee. Oh! Don't
          forget to tell me how everything
          goes. They up'ed their security a
          bit, so be careful. Or don't.
          Prison's nice. I'll see you soon,
          mama.

INT. AIRPLANE - DAY

Tre, now sporting a pair of aviator glasses himself, smiles
and laughs as he looks over at Hazel--who's having the time
of her life and Ms. Joy--who is deathly panicking in the
copilot seat.

                    JOY
          Tre, baby, don't you do anything
          foolish now, WHOA!

Tre tilts the plane down, taking a playful dive.

EXT. SKY - DAY

                    JOY (V.O.)
          You land this plane right now, you
          hear?!

                    TRE (V.O.)
          Happy birthday, Ms. Joy!

                    JOY (V.O.)
          You're gonna sleep on the porch
          tonight!

THE SHOOTING SCRIPT

The plane drifts gently away, into a sea of dreamy clouds.

FADE TO BLACK.

www.ingramcontent.com/pod-product-compliance
Lightning Source LLC
Chambersburg PA
CBHW010744310726
48971CB00010B/2950